"When is yo...
Delaney ask...

"November." Rac... and Delaney found himself wanting to do the same.

"November. That's a nice time to have a baby," he muttered. If she wasn't sitting in a jail cell at the time. He was liking this assignment less and less. Or was it that he was liking his suspect more and more?

"Do you have any children?" Rachel asked curiously.

"Children?" Delaney's brow furrowed. Were children part of his cover story or not? "Uh, no. I'm not married," he said hastily.

"Neither am I," Rachel said softly.

That's it, Delaney, put your foot in it! "Look… I'm sorry."

Rachel patted his arm. "It's okay. It could be worse. I could have married that two-timing bastard," she said bitterly.

Delaney studied her troubled expression. Was he gazing into the face of a murderer? He knew from experience that murderers came in every size, shape and colour. Not too many of them, though, looked as good as Rachel Hart. It would be a hell of a lot easier if his suspect looked like Whistler's mother, and acted like a first-class bitch instead of being so damn sexy and appealing.

Dear Reader

Talented Temptation author Elise Title has
written another funny, sexy mini-series in the
vein of the popular Fortune Brothers. The Hart
Girls follows the ups and downs of three feisty,
independent sisters who work at a TV station in
Pittsville, New York.

In *Dangerous at Heart*, a dumbfounded Rachel
Hart can't believe she's a suspect in her ex-
fiancé's death. She only dumped Nelson—she
didn't bump him off! Sexy, hard-edged cop
Delaney Parker must uncover the truth—or bring
Rachel in.

Look for Julie Hart's story in *Heartstruck* in
September 1995. Kate Hart's tale, *Heart to
Heart,* completes this wonderful trilogy in
October 1995. Happy reading!

The Editor
Mills & Boon Temptation
Eton House
18-24 Paradise Road
Richmond
Surrey
TW9 1SR

DANGEROUS AT HEART

BY

ELISE TITLE

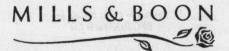

MILLS & BOON

All the characters in this book have no existence outside the imagination of the author, and have no relation whatsoever to anyone bearing the same name or names. They are not even distantly inspired by any individual known or unknown to the author, and all the incidents are pure invention.

MILLS & BOON and the Rose Device are trademarks of the publisher. TEMPTATION is a trademark of Harlequin Enterprises Limited, used under licence.
This edition published by arrangement with Harlequin Enterprises II B.V. First published in Great Britain in 1995 by Harlequin Mills & Boon Limited, Eton House, 18-24 Paradise Road, Richmond, Surrey TW9 1SR

© Elise Title 1994

ISBN 0 263 79366 4

21 - 9508

Printed in Great Britain by BPC Paperbacks Ltd

Prologue

March 12

Aunt Julie sent me this journal last Christmas so I could keep an accounting of "my life and times"—as Aunt Julie put it. Okay, I've been meaning to start writing, but the truth is there's been nothing much to say about my life and times, what with being twelve years old and living up here in the boonies in Pittsville, New York. Aunt Julie, on the other hand, lives an incredibly exciting life. She's a big-shot television anchor on "News and Views" in Washington, DC. She's interviewed the president. Twice. And the hip political rapper, Poli Sci, right after he led this big demonstration against music censorship in front of the Lincoln Memorial. She even got me his autograph. Which I have hung up on my wall right next to my Bon Jovi poster and a signed photo of Jordan Hammond.

Jordan Hammond is Aunt Julie's coanchor and he's a real hunk. Aunt Julie's nuts about him. Mom doesn't like him much, though. One time she was talking to my Aunt Rachel who lives in New York City and I heard her say she wouldn't trust Jordan Hammond as far as she could throw him. Truth is, Mom's opinion of most men isn't all that great.

You could say Aunt Julie's my idol. She's just so tough and never lets those big shots she's always interviewing on her show get away with anything. Like when I was out there visiting her in the fall and I confessed I'd like to do what she's doing someday. She sat me right down and gave me some pointers. Always do your homework, she said. Check your leads. Get the lowdown. And then once you have all the facts, go for the jugular. Never back down. Never let them intimidate you. She talks like that. I can't wait to visit Aunt Julie again. She says maybe I can come in the summer.

I'm always up for going off someplace exciting, although I will admit it's not too bad here in the summer when all the fancy out-of-towners come swarming in here to see the summer-stock plays, visit the artsy-tartsy galleries, and spend oodles of money in the boutiques. It's real lively then. The rest of the year, though, it's the pits! Get it? Pittsville. The pits? My mom hates when I say that. She loves it out here. I ask her, "How can you love it here? It's so boring." She gives me this lopsided smile and says, "Boring? If only that were true."

I guess life is a little more exciting for my mom, what with her owning her own TV station. WPIT in the heart of the Berkshire Mountains broadcasting in half-a-dozen towns in upstate New York and neighboring Massachusetts. My dad used to own it, but she got it when they divorced. My dad got Sue Ellen—his secretary. They're married now and have twin boys. Little monsters. Mom says it serves him right. She isn't too fond of my dad. They used to fight a lot, especially after she found out about Sue Ellen. I'm not supposed to know that she knew Dad was cheating on her when they were still married, so, to make her happy, I pretend I didn't know. Even though it was the talk of the town. One thing about living in a place like Pittsville—everybody always knows your business, sometimes even before you do.

Personally, I never could stand Sue Ellen, and I think my mom's a lot prettier even if she doesn't have "a set of knockers on her." That's how I overheard Gus, the cameraman at the station, describe Sue Ellen to his assistant, Joe. I overhear a lot of things on the chance that one of these days I'll hear something interesting. I'm dying for something interesting to happen in my life. Things were pretty "interesting" for a while after my folks got divorced three years back and Dad was still in town. I guess you could say I got spoiled rotten by my dad. Mom says it was his guilty conscience.

I don't see much of my dad anymore, now that he and Sue Ellen and their bratty boys moved to Cleveland. I did spend three days of my Christmas holiday with them, but my dad was working the whole time and Sue Ellen was shopping the whole time, so mostly I got stuck with the brats. Some holiday! I couldn't wait to come home to Pittsville. That's how bad it was.

My mom and I are real tight, although I do think it would be good for her if she could find a man. She hasn't dated anyone since she and Dad split up. She says she's got her hands full, raising me and running WPIT.

My best friends, Alice and Nadine, think it's so neat that my mom runs the only TV station in the area. I guess so, but it's not like we have any real big-time

shows or anything. Mostly, we run repeats of old sit-
coms like "Gilligan's Island," "The Partridge Family,"
and "Mr. Ed." I'm sorry, but I just can't buy a talking
horse. Then there are these dumb infomercials—everything from some muscle-bound goon pitching thigh
and tummy trimmers to old sitcom stars trying to sell
you hair-care products, diet programs and spiritual-
fulfillment videotapes. Mom thinks they're dumb, too,
but like she says, "They help pay the bills." My mom
worries a lot about money and problems at the station.

There is one fun part of running a TV station. We do
put on some "live" shows. My favorite's Ben Sandler's
"Pittsville Patter," which is sort of a cross between
Oprah and Jay Leno, only Ben never gets to interview
anyone really bizarre or really famous. Still, it's a pretty
good show and Ben's our local celebrity. Alice and Nadine both have crushes on him. He is kind of good-
looking, but he's always been like a big brother to me.
Ben also does the local news at six and eleven with his
coanchor, Alan Munch, who owns the ice-cream shop
in town.

Then there's Meg Cromwell's cooking show,
"Cooking With Meg." I once made the mistake of
showing up at the station right in the middle of her
show and she called me into the studio to taste her Bean
Pudding Cromwell. Oh my God, I never tasted anything that awful in my whole life. I really thought I
would puke, right on the air. I'd have been a total
laughingstock, since practically everyone in town
watches the show. Somehow I managed to hold it
down. It was a miracle. My mother said I was a terrific

actress, but I thought she was just trying to make me feel better until Mrs. Cromwell gave me the whole pot of that gross goop to take home—"seeing as how I liked it so much."

I'm almost forgetting that there is an actual reason I started writing in my journal on this particular day. The thing is, I have this feeling that something's about to happen. There've been an awful lot of phone calls these past few days, back and forth, between my mom and Aunt Julie, and my mom and Aunt Rachel. Too bad Aunt Julie bought my mom a cordless phone for Christmas. Now, whenever Mom's talking and doesn't want me to "overhear," she takes the phone into the bathroom. Even runs the water sometimes, which is a sure sign something's up.

But what? I tried to quiz my mom but she gave me one of her looks that mean she thinks I'm too young to know what's going on.

Which is why I figure it's got to have something to do with S-E-X.

March 15

You won't believe it. There I was, brushing my teeth in the bathroom, minding my own business—for once— and I hear my mom gasping as she's walking down the hall, clutching the cordless phone to her ear. She heads for the kitchen. I head for the laundry room, which is right next to the kitchen. If she sees me in there I can always say I'm looking for my blue turtleneck, which is the truth. I've been looking for it for two weeks.

My mom's on the phone with Aunt Julie and she's talking about Aunt Rachel. Well, actually she's talking about Aunt Rachel's fiancé, Nelson Lang. Mom is saying to Aunt Julie that Aunt Rachel's problem is that she's always been too much of a romantic, and that she's never exactly had good judgment when it came to men.

Personally, I can't see how anyone could ever feel romantic about someone called Nelson. With a name like that, I wasn't the least bit surprised that he worked for a bird-watching magazine. I just can't picture Aunt Rachel with a nerdy bird-watcher. She's my mom's kid sister and she's so beautiful. I mean my mom's pretty in a "mom" sort of way, and Aunt Julie's pretty in a classy *Ms. Magazine*-woman sort of way, but Aunt Rachel looks like a movie star. Kind of a cross between Michelle Pfeiffer and Cindy Crawford, only with real curly auburn hair. What I wouldn't give for hair like that . . .

So, anyway, there I am, scrounging around in the laundry room—can you believe it? I actually found that blue turtleneck—and I hear Mom saying to Aunt Julie how she never believed for one minute that Nelson was telling Aunt Rachel the truth about being a writer for a bird-watchers' magazine. I didn't think too much of it, because like I said, my mom thinks most men pretty much lie when it suits them. But then I hear her say that it doesn't surprise her one bit that he works for the mob.

Works for the mob? I couldn't have heard right. Nelson Lang a mobster? But there didn't seem to be any argument coming from Aunt Julie's end of the line. So it must be true. Nelson Lang must really be a gangster.

Well, I will never again jump to conclusions where names are concerned.

After my mom hung up with Aunt Julie, she called Aunt Rachel. I was still in the laundry room and it was almost eight and I knew if I stuck around much longer, I'd be late for school.

Oh, what the hell. How many times in my life is something this exciting going to happen here in Pittsville? I pulled a load of laundry out of the dryer and started folding it to be doing something that would help out my mom and also so I wouldn't feel so guilty about eavesdropping, not to mention a late demerit at school. Aunt Rachel must have been real upset when my mom got her on the line, because my mom used that same soothing voice she always uses with me when I'm real upset. After a few minutes, though, Mom did say a little gruffly how she wasn't surprised that Nelson was a no-account racketeer. I bet if Aunt Rachel had told Mom that Nelson was also an ax murderer who escaped from a prison, Mom would have said, "Doesn't surprise me."

And that's not the half of it. Here's the real kicker. Aunt Rachel is *pregnant*. Mom kept saying to Aunt Rachel, "Are you sure? Are you absolutely certain?" Mom must have been convinced, because she immediately went into her take-charge mode. That's my mom. Whenever there's a "problem" or a "situation," she believes you've "got to get a handle on it," and "do whatever's got to be done."

So, Aunt Rachel's coming home to Pittsville to stay with us. Mom's going to make her sales manager at the station, since the job just came open anyway. Morey

Lewis was sales manager, but he and his son, Josh, bought a new fast-food restaurant just a few doors down from the station. I don't think Mom's holding out any great hopes for Aunt Rachel as sales manager, but then Morey wasn't exactly supersuccessful at getting advertisers himself. Now he promises to buy some time for his Chicken Coop, so Aunt Rachel will start off with one new local advertiser. The real bucks, though, come from ad companies in New York City, and my mom told Aunt Rachel she could hire a sales rep.

Things are really going to pick up around here now. I just know it. I wonder if they'll do a TV movie about Aunt Rachel's life and times as a mobster's girlfriend. I'll talk to Aunt Julie about it. She's coming home next weekend. I guess she and mom want to do whatever they can to cheer up poor Aunt Rachel. That's the neat thing about sisters. You can count on them to be there for you in a pinch. I wish I had sisters to be there for me in a pinch. It's a drag being an only child. Still, it's great having such neat aunts.

Hey, I just realized. Now I'm going to be an aunt. I can't believe it. This is so great. . . .

1

RACHEL HART WRAPPED herself in her sister's terry robe as she sat cross-legged in the center of the bed in Kate's spare bedroom. Her auburn hair was still damp from her shower, slowly drying into ringlets that seemed to have a life of their own. She wound her arms around her knees, hugging them to her chest. All she really wanted to do was curl up under the covers and go to sleep. She'd arrived in Pittsville at five o'clock in the morning, having only managed a catnap during the four-hour train ride from Manhattan.

Fighting back a yawn, Rachel gave Kate a wan look. "He seemed truly knowledgeable about birds. He could even imitate the chirp of a spotted sandpiper."

Kate rolled her eyes as she sat on the window seat across from the bed, her elbows on her knees, her hands propping up her chin. She, too, was exhausted, having gotten little more sleep than Rachel.

"How would you know how a spotted sandpiper sounded, Rach? Have you ever seen one, much less heard one chirp? For all you know, they don't even make a peep." Kate's tone was more frustrated than angry. How could Rachel, at twenty-five, be so gullible? Kate started blaming herself and Julie, who had both teased their kid sister unmercifully when they were all little because it had always been so easy to pull Rachel's leg.

Seeing Rachel's pained expression, Kate cursed herself for sounding so cynical. Not that she didn't feel cynical, especially when it came to that creep, Nelson Lang. But what Rachel needed now was a little TLC. She went over to the bed and reached out to her sister, taking hold of her hand. "How did you find out that Nelson wasn't the art director of *Bird-watchers' Weekly?*"

Rachel pulled a tissue out of her pocket and dabbed at her brown eyes, absently tucking some runaway curls behind her ears. "I didn't exactly find out he wasn't the art director," she said, sniffing. "I found out there was no such magazine as *Bird-watchers' Weekly.* What happened was, Nelson was out of town. On a—" she paused, keeping her eyes averted from Kate "—bird-watching expedition for the magazine, and I wanted to get word to him that I . . . that my take-home test came out . . . positive. I was so excited, and I wanted to tell Nelson right away that I was . . . pregnant."

"How did he take it?" Kate asked, her tone gentler than before.

"He didn't," Rachel replied. "I . . . I couldn't get in touch with him. I thought I'd call the magazine and see if they could give me a number where Nelson could be reached. Nelson had written down the number of the magazine on a slip of paper—at least, he told me it was the number of the magazine—but I'd misplaced it. You know how I am about losing things."

Kate smiled faintly. She remembered how everyone in the family would always tell Rachel that if her head wasn't attached, she'd probably lose that, too.

Rachel blew her nose. "So, I called Information. There was no listing for *Bird-watchers' Weekly.* I started searching through the apartment for that slip of paper with the number on it, and that's when I found—" This time she came to a complete stop.

"Found what?"

Rachel looked down at the old-fashioned white chenille spread covering the bed. "His gun." Her voice was just above a whisper.

"Lots of people own guns, Rachel."

"With silencers?" Rachel added glumly.

Kate felt an icy chill zigzag down her spine. A silencer-fitted gun was another story.

"And that wasn't all," Rachel said, her hands cupping her still-flat stomach. She was just six weeks pregnant and hadn't begun to show. Yet. Still, she could feel life growing inside her and she already felt an attachment. Even with everything that had happened, there was one thing of which she was certain: She wanted this baby.

Kate was disturbed by Rachel's pallor. She remembered the early stages of her own pregnancy with Skye. It had been such a happy time for her and Arnie. Probably the happiest time of their marriage. Her heart went out to her little sister. Twenty-five, single, pregnant, the poor kid's father a mobster, no less. Well, at least Rachel had her and the rest of the Hart clan. They'd see her through.

"What else?" Kate asked.

Rachel really didn't want to go into the "what else," but she knew her sister would keep pressing until she told her everything. "I found papers. Business papers. Reports. Letters. Not the sort of stuff an art director at a bird-watching magazine would have. I read a few of the letters. Some of them made me...uneasy." One, in particular, that she'd read had been downright devastating. She shut her eyes. She was beginning to feel a little queasy. Morning sickness, she guessed, although it could be the topic of discussion that was turning her stomach.

"Saltines," Kate said decisively.

Rachel gave her sister a perplexed look as she watched her leap off the bed. "Saltines?" Where did crackers fit into this?

Kate was already opening the bedroom door and calling out to Skye, who was down in the kitchen eating her breakfast, to bring up a box of saltine crackers from the cupboard.

A minute later Skye dashed upstairs. Her mother took the box from her at the door. "You'd better hurry or you'll be late for school."

Skye sighed and reluctantly trudged off to her room for her book bag.

Kate closed the door and took a few crackers from the box, handing them over to her sister. "Here. Eat these."

"I don't think I can," Rachel protested.

"They'll settle your stomach. Trust me. I lived on saltines the first three months I was pregnant with Skye. Sometimes, that was all I could get down, and keep down."

Rachel dutifully nibbled on the crackers. After downing three of them she did feel a little better, and even managed a weak smile.

Kate smiled back. "Okay. Go on with your sad tale."

Rachel sighed. "A little man in a blue serge suit came to see me at the apartment the next day. Mr. Kelso. Albert Kelso. From the . . . FBI."

Kate squinted at her sister. "How did you know he was from the FBI? No, wait. He hummed the national anthem."

Rachel threw a pillow at Kate. "Will you give me a break, here?"

"I was only teasing. Sorry," Kate said contritely.

"It's okay," Rachel told her, but she found herself fighting back tears. It wasn't anything Kate had said. Kate was just being Kate. Rachel didn't doubt for one instant that her sister cared deeply about her predicament. Make that predicaments. It was just that she'd been so emotional lately. Well, she'd always been emotional, but she was more emotional now than usual.

Kate saw Rachel's eyes get misty. "It's all that creep Nelson's fault. Boy, if I could get my hands on him . . ."

"He showed me his photo ID. It was very official," Rachel said.

"Nelson?"

"No. Albert Kelso."

"It could have been a phony ID. How do you know for sure it wasn't one of Nelson's mobster pals?"

Some color came back into Rachel's cheeks. She tossed her head back, her patrician jaw jutting out defiantly. "I know you think I'm a complete ninny, but I'm not. I called the FBI right as I was staring at Mr. Kelso.

They confirmed his employment with them and even gave me a very accurate description of him, right down to a mole on his right cheek."

"Did he have to drop his pants?"

Rachel laughed, despite herself. Leave it to Kate to cheer her up even when she felt like her world was falling apart.

"What did this Mr. Kelso with the mole on his right cheek want?" Kate asked, relieved to see Rachel brighten a little. Something told her Rachel was going to need plenty more laughs to make it through the next seven or eight months without coming unglued.

"He asked me if I knew that Nelson had been before a grand jury two years ago on racketeering charges, only they didn't have enough on him to get an indictment." She hesitated, blanching. "Mr. Kelso told me one of the key witnesses for the state had an accident the very morning of the hearing."

Kate's throat went dry. "An accident?"

"He was hit by a car while he was crossing Third Avenue. He . . . died."

There was a long silence, both sisters thinking the same thing. A very convenient "accident."

"I told Mr. Kelso, of course I didn't know anything about Nelson having been brought up before a grand jury," Rachel went on. She gave her sister a downcast look. "I was absolutely horrified. I only knew at that point that Nelson wasn't who he'd told me he was, and that he might have gotten caught up in something not quite . . . kosher. But a grand jury investigation on racketeering charges? Nelson?" She sighed. Why did she always take people at their word? Especially men?

"Mr. Kelso didn't seem to believe me that I knew nothing about it. I explained that I'd only met Nelson a little over nine months ago, and that before then I'd been working as a research assistant at a lab in Boston so I wasn't even in New York when this grand-jury thing happened."

"What else did he tell you about Nelson?" Kate asked.

"He didn't tell me anything," Rachel said. "He started asking me a lot of questions about Nelson's activities, his friends, his . . . business acquaintances. I kept trying to explain that Nelson and I led a very quiet life. We almost never had anyone over to the house, and when we went out—to a movie or a show or for a bite—we always went alone. Nelson was very shy and retiring. Very sweet, gentle . . ."

Rachel remembered sitting there in Nelson's Central Park West apartment while this funny-looking little man with wire-rimmed glasses, thinning brown hair, and a mole just under his left eye, threw question after question at her—the implication clear in each and every one of them that Nelson Lang was considered by the FBI to be a truly nefarious character. Just the day before, she'd found out she was going to have a baby and she was on top of the world. Then she'd found those papers and those letters. Twenty-four hours later, sitting there with Albert Kelso from the FBI, Rachel felt like her whole world had collapsed. Trying to be optimistic, she decided there was nowhere else to go from here but up.

Kate could see the raw pain and fear in her sister's face. She was very worried about Rachel's emotional and physical state. "You must be exhausted. Why don't you get some sleep and we'll talk more later."

Kate started to rise, but Rachel took hold of her wrist.

"Do you think I should have given Mr. Kelso those papers and records I found?"

"Why didn't you give them to him?" Kate asked.

The truth was, Rachel had kept hoping that somehow it was all some horrible misunderstanding—a case of mistaken identity. Nelson would come home and would convince her that they had the wrong man. God, she might even have believed him. Or she had desperately wanted to. Only how could he ever have explained away one of the letters she'd read?

"I felt I owed it to Nelson to talk to him first," Rachel answered quietly.

Kate opened her mouth to say something, but shut it again.

"We talked, all right," Rachel said tightly, shivering as she remembered her encounter with Nelson when he returned from his "bird-watching expedition" two days earlier. "It was awful. Here I was, the one who'd discovered all of these . . . dreadful things about him, and he was the one who was angry at me. As if it was my fault the FBI were looking into his . . . activities. The worst part was, he didn't deny a thing. He . . . he actually laughed at me when I told him I believed he was exactly who he'd told me he was. He assumed it simply made me feel better to . . . to pretend. He said he couldn't believe anyone could truly be so . . . naive."

"Did you tell him you were pregnant?" Kate asked gently.

Rachel shook her head vehemently. "No. No, I couldn't. I fell in love with a bird lover, not a racketeer. Once it finally sank in that everything Nelson ever told me about himself was a lie, I realized he was really a complete stranger to me. All my feelings for him vanished. I didn't know this man at all. I couldn't tell him about the baby. I was afraid. I didn't know how he'd react or what he'd do."

Kate put her arm protectively around her sister. "You did the right thing. He doesn't deserve to know about the baby. You're going to be fine. It's all going to work out." She hoped.

Rachel pressed her head to Kate's shoulder. "I knew I had to get away from him, but it took me a day to get up my nerve. By last night I was at the breaking point. I waited until I was certain he was fast asleep and then I snuck out of the apartment in the dead of night. I was going to call you first, Kate, to let you know I was on my way, but I only just caught the last train out here. I hated waking you so early in the morning to come get me at the train station. I was too upset to even think to call a cab."

Kate frowned. Something was troubling her.

Rachel looked up. "What is it, Kate?"

"I'm just trying to think how we should handle it if Nelson comes here looking for you." She hesitated. "I think we ought to call this Mr. Kelso at the FBI and—"

"No," Rachel said fiercely, clutching at Kate. "No. I swore to Nelson I'd never say a word to the FBI. Nelson said . . . if I knew what was good for me . . . I'd keep my word. Don't you see?" she continued, her voice full of desperation and panic. "It isn't just me now. It's me and the baby."

Kate immediately thought of that key witness who'd conveniently gotten run over right before he was to appear before the grand jury. Rachel was right. She could be placing both herself and her baby in jeopardy. Kate had to figure something else out.

"Anyway, Nelson believes I don't know anything about his real activities," Rachel said. "I didn't tell him about those papers I'd found and I'm sure he's moved them out of the apartment by now."

"He might want you back, Rachel," Kate said quietly. Few men had ever given her beautiful sister up easily.

Tears spilled down Rachel's cheeks. "No, he won't."

She said it so emphatically that Kate was taken aback. "Why not?"

"One of the letters I found in Nelson's desk drawer was from . . . another woman."

Men, Kate thought. They were all alike. No matter how green their own lawn was, they always thought the grass was greener on some other one.

"It was a . . . very passionate letter. All about how she couldn't wait until he'd finally . . . dumped me so that they could be together all the time." Rachel dropped her head in her hands. "The bastard was two-timing me. I thought we were going to get married. I thought we were going to raise a family together. I thought he loved me. I thought he loved . . . birds. Lies. All lies. I will never trust another man as long as I live."

Kate gently rubbed her sister's back. Now if only she could believe that Rachel meant that, half her problems would be licked. Of course, there was still the other half....

LIGHTS WERE FLASHING and there was a familiar hum in the air as Delaney Parker stepped into the large, beautifully appointed kitchen of apartment 17A at 321 Central Park West. He got a few nods from some of New York's finest as they went about their work. The coroner, Daniel Flynn, a burly fellow with a shock of red hair, was kneeling on the shiny white tile floor next to the body. He looked up at the new arrival.

Delaney flashed him a smile. The coroner nodded. "Your boss is having a powwow with a fellow from the FBI. You want to go find him?"

"He'll find me," Delaney said with no inflection as he looked down at the dead man lying in a heap on the cold tile floor, the cherrywood handle of a kitchen knife protruding from the upper right quadrant of his back. He was dressed in a Paisley-print silk dressing gown. A thin rivulet of dried red blood threaded its way down the back of the robe and then detoured left because of the curve of the body, trickling onto the white tile. The spots of blood on the floor looked a little like dried catsup from a sloppy eater.

A police photographer popped out his used flash bulb and nodded to the coroner. "All done here. I'll get the roll developed and have the shots on your desk by four."

"Who found him?" Delaney asked as the coroner got to his feet.

"I did," came a vaguely familiar voice from across the kitchen.

Delaney turned to see Albert Kelso from the FBI enter the room and walk over to the refrigerator. Delaney had met with Kelso a number of times during the past few years over a variety of cases. Most recently, Kelso had been making inquiries into the underworld activities of Nelson Lang, a mobster well-known to the New York boys in blue. Lang had been frustrating the cops and the government fellows for years. They all knew he was a major player in the rackets, but they'd never gotten enough on him to nail him.

"Got all your prints?" Kelso asked, as everyone started packing up and the boys from the morgue set about loading the dead man onto the stretcher, chest down so as not to disturb the knife wound. One of the detectives nodded and the little man grabbed the chrome handle of the fridge and opened the door, giving the well-stocked shelves a quick check before pulling out a container of vanilla yogurt. After three tries he found the silverware drawer and removed a shiny silver spoon.

"What? No breakfast this morning?" Delaney asked Kelso, turning from the FBI agent to catch a brief glimpse of the corpse's face as he was lifted from the floor. Nelson Lang wasn't wearing his typical cocky, "You boys can't touch me and you know it" expression now. Delaney wasn't sure what the look on his face meant. Surprise? Anger? Indignation? Maybe a little of all three, he decided. Nelson Lang was one of those sociopathic types who thought he was invincible. *Guess again, Nelson,* Delaney said to himself.

Kelso was finishing up his late-morning snack as everyone but Delaney cleared out of the kitchen.

"There's another yogurt in the fridge if you want," Kelso said. "Prune whip."

Delaney grinned. "I'll pass."

"Thought you might," Kelso replied, ambling over to a kitchen stool at the built-in counter eating space that ran halfway down one wall of the long, narrow room. The whole kitchen was painted stark white, but there was a series of colorful framed travel posters on the walls between banks of hanging cupboards, also white with glass doors.

"So, you discovered the body," Delaney said.

"I was here a few days ago," Kelso said, after swallowing a spoonful of yogurt. "Lang was out of town and I had a little talk with his live-in girlfriend, Rachel Hart. Only I did most of the talking. She wasn't exactly loquacious. I came back this morning to see if I could persuade her to be a little more forthcoming."

Delaney plucked an apple out of a pretty brown-and-blue pottery bowl on the counter and shined it up on his brown leather bomber jacket. "Where is the girlfriend?"

Kelso craned his neck, rubbing it with the back of his hand. "Gone. No one answered the door when I got here. I let myself in, thinking I might have a little look around. That's when I discovered Lang. As for the girlfriend, not only wasn't she around, but all her clothes were gone. Guess she isn't planning on coming back."

"Not too surprising," Delaney reflected, as his gaze fell on the faint splatter of dried blood on the tile floor. "You think she did it?"

"If you're asking me do I think she had the means, motive and opportunity, you're damned straight, Delaney."

Comprehending the girlfriend's means and opportunity presented no problem for the ten-year police veteran. Motive was another thing. "Why would she want to off him?"

"Why do most women want to kill their boyfriends or husbands or whatever?" Homicide Chief Louis Mendez asked, as he stepped into the kitchen to join the two men. Mendez was a lean, wiry man in his early forties. His trademark half-spent cigarette was dangling from his lips, and a dusting of ashes sprinkled down the front of his open gray jacket.

Delaney smiled at his chief. He didn't have to give his answer much thought. "Jealousy."

"Hell hath no fury, blah, blah, blah," Kelso deadpanned as he tidily tossed the finished yogurt container into the trash masher whose prior contents had already been carted off by the police for further checking, then rinsed and dried off his spoon, returning it to its proper resting place.

Delaney munched on a bite of apple, waving the rest of it in Kelso's direction. "I presume you know something specific that makes you believe she was jealous."

Kelso glanced over at Mendez, then pulled out a folded letter from the inside pocket of his blue serge jacket.

Delaney took it and read it, his eyebrows slowly rising. "So the bastard was cheating on her. How do you know she read it?"

"Fingerprints match those all around the house," Kelso said.

"It's a neat, tidy case, for a change. Jealous girlfriend in a fit of rage stabs lover in the back, grabs her belongings and hightails it out of town faster than you can say Jackie Robinson," Mendez said, puffing on his cigarette as Kelso reclaimed the letter and deposited it back into his pocket.

"Maybe it's *too* neat and tidy," Delaney said, often finding himself playing the devil's advocate with his boss. "This gal who wrote the love letter—Suzanne— what if she came up to see Lang late last night after his live-in girlfriend was asleep and Lang told her he'd had a change of heart and planned to keep the status quo? She could have stabbed him in the back. The girlfriend—Rachel—maybe hears something, goes into the kitchen, sees Lang dead on the floor, maybe even spots the killer and ducks out, panicked. Then she waits until she's sure the other gal's left and she packs up and runs away, knowing that she's likely to be the one accused of murdering the creep."

Mendez shrugged. "You always can be relied upon to tell a good story, Delaney. But it's pretty farfetched."

"I agree with your boss," Kelso said. "When I did talk to Lang's girlfriend, I was convinced she was holding out on me. You boys need to investigate the Hart woman as the star suspect in Lang's murder. That part's strictly in your domain. But the Bureau stands to gain here, too, Delaney. During the course of your investigation, you might be able to uncover some other information that could be useful to us. Nelson Lang was only one cog in a very well-run syndicate wheel. If Rachel Hart ends up facing a murder rap, she might be persuaded to work a plea-bargaining deal if she's willing to cooperate, and give us a few leads to some of the other significant cogs."

"We're jumping the gun here. The first order of business is to track down this Rachel Hart," Delaney said, finishing off his apple.

"Oh, that won't be necessary," Kelso said amiably. "We already know where she is. In Pittsville, New York."

Delaney grimaced. "Pittsville?" He'd never heard of the place, but it didn't sound very promising. He was strictly a big-city boy and he didn't fancy having to go undercover in some two-bit town—with a name like Pittsville, no less.

"It's a quaint little touch of Americana in upstate New York right in the heart of the Berkshire Mountains," Kelso said. "Unfortunately, it's mud season right now so you won't be seeing it at its best. As for Rachel Hart, though, you'll have no complaints. She's real easy on the eyes."

"What you're telling me here," Delaney said, addressing both men, "is that you have nothing solid on her. No fingerprints on the knife, for instance. No hard evidence to be able to press charges on her."

"The knife handle was wiped clean. I said she was pretty. I didn't say she was stupid," was Kelso's retort.

Mendez slipped a photo out of his pocket that he'd removed from a silver frame on the piano in the living room. "See for yourself."

Delaney took a look at the photo. A long look. Either Rachel Hart photographed real well or she was one of the most beautiful women he'd ever laid eyes on. Which only meant one thing to Delaney. It was going to make his job, which was difficult under the best of circumstances, all the more difficult.

"You really think she did it, huh?" Delaney mused, having trouble taking his eyes from the photo.

"I had hoped to persuade Miss Hart to be a star witness against Lang," Kelso said. "Now that Lang's dead, she's gone from being a prospective star witness to being your star suspect."

"We don't want her running scared, so I'm not going to have her brought in for questioning," Mendez said. "Besides, she's out of town and we'd have to go through a lot of pain-in-the-ass rigmarole to get her back here. We'll send a couple of plainclothes boys out to question her in Pittsville. Once Lang's death hits the news, she'll think it's fishy if someone doesn't show up to get a statement from her. I don't have high hopes they'll get anything out of her, though."

"You mean like a confession?" Delaney quipped.

"I'm leaving that to you," Mendez said glibly, eyeing the six-foot-two, ruggedly handsome undercover cop with his sandy blond hair and savvy gray-green eyes. "I don't know why it is, but women are like putty in your hands, Delaney."

Mendez was exaggerating, but it was true that most women found Delaney Parker attractive. Even granted that a few had been putty in his hands, they'd been more of a turnoff to Delaney, who preferred women who were as tough, independent and self-sufficient as he was. At the same time he wanted a woman who was tender, gentle and sensitive. A tall order. Which was probably why he was still a bachelor.

One of these days, though, if the right woman came along, Delaney thought he wouldn't mind tossing in the towel. He'd gotten into this line of work almost ten years ago, looking for adventure, danger, excitement. Now, he was thirty-six years old and he'd tasted more than his fair share of all three. What he hadn't bargained for was the loneliness, the feeling of being unattached and disconnected from the world that also came with the territory. He was getting ready to settle down, have a family. He smiled to himself. Hey, did men have a biological clock, too?

Again, Delaney's gaze dropped, to the photo of Rachel Hart. It was a close-up of her tanned face, which was framed by a voluptuous tangle of shoulder-length reddish brown curls. Her thickly lashed eyes were the color of bittersweet chocolate. She was smiling into the camera with this real innocent, dreamy look.

Delaney shook his head in wonder. What was a lovely young thing like her doing with a sleazeball like Nelson Lang? Maybe, she'd finally come to her senses and wanted out. Maybe Nelson didn't want to let her go. There could have been a row. She could have picked up that kitchen knife and stabbed him in self-defense.

In the back?

Delaney scowled. Was he going soft in his advancing years?

"Rachel's staying with her sister, Kate Hart, right in the center of town," Kelso was saying, flipping open a little notepad on which he'd jotted down the pertinent data purloined from a long series of FBI bugged telephone conversations that had, for the most part, proved disappointingly uninformative. "Kate owns the local TV station in town. WPIT. She's making Rachel her sales manager."

"We thought we'd have you apply for a job at the station as a television sales rep," Mendez said.

"A what?" Delaney had played a lot of roles in his seven years undercover, but a television sales rep? It seemed to him that had to be about one notch above TV repairman.

"Hey," Mendez said breezily, "you know, you sell TV time to the ad agencies. Mostly in New York. In order to put on shows, the station's got to sell advertising time. That's the department Rachel Hart will be heading. We'll get a top agency in town and they'll fill you in on the details of the job, and back you up all the way."

"And what makes you think Rachel Hart's going to hire me to do this job?" Delaney retorted.

Mendez grinned. "You've never failed us before. Besides, we'll have an impressive résumé whipped up for you. That, and your irresistible charm, and you're a shoo-in," Mendez assured him. "And it's a perfect cover, because it gives you a built-in excuse to go back and forth between Pittsville and here, meaning we can stay in close touch."

"Selling TV time, huh?"

"Stop looking so skeptical," Mendez said. "It's gonna be a piece of cake."

Delaney wasn't convinced. "A piece of cake? I don't even own a television set, Mendez. The last show I think I saw on TV except for an occasional football

game at Murphy's Bar was some dumb show called
'Sledge Hammer' about this idiot cop who made Dirty
Harry look like Howdy Doody. That was like eight
years ago. I saw the show once. Once was enough."

Kelso chuckled. "I watched that show a few times. It
wasn't that bad."

Mendez walked over and patted Delaney on the
shoulder. "You're a quick study, Del. What are you
worried about?"

Delaney smiled wryly. "Did I say I was worried?"

"One thing I did fail to mention," Kelso said as the
undercover cop cum TV sales rep started to leave. "Rachel Hart is pregnant."

Delaney stopped dead in his tracks. "Now I'm worried."

March 28

Poor Aunt Rachel. The worst thing has happened.
Nelson Lang is dead! Murdered! It made front-page
headlines in all the big-city papers. Even the *Berkshire
Press* ran the story. It was on CNN and all the network
news channels. Aunt Rachel's name was mentioned as
Nelson's "love interest." The whole town is buzzing.

Two cops from New York City came up here to question her. Of course, I wasn't supposed to know they
were cops. They weren't in uniform or anything, but
they didn't fool me or anyone else in town.

Aunt Rachel was an absolute wreck even at the very
possibility that she could be a suspect in Nelson's murder. It's so ridiculous. How could anyone in their right
mind think she's a murderer? Aunt Rachel wouldn't

hurt a fly, much less stab Nelson Lang in the back. Obviously, the cops agreed, because they didn't arrest her or anything.

It had to be one of his mobster friends. Or a hit man. You see it on TV all the time. The murder had to have taken place after Aunt Rachel left their apartment. Like she told the cops, Nelson was completely alive, snoring in his bed, when she took off. Okay, so I happened to overhear snips of conversation while I was painting an old bookcase in the basement, which just happened to be near a heating vent that ran up to the living room.

I felt just awful when I heard Aunt Rachel crying, and you can bet my mom put her two cents in, telling those cops that they had no business coming here in the first place.

Later, I was at Mack's General Store—buying more boxes of saltine crackers—and I overheard my *one-time* best friend, Alice, telling this jerk in our class, Billy Seager, that she'd seen this movie on TV where someone just like Aunt Rachel had killed her boyfriend and everyone thought at first that she was just too sweet and innocent to be the murderer. I darted out of the aisle and threw the box of saltines right at her. Oh, she tried to apologize, saying she didn't mean that she thought Aunt Rachel had killed that awful Nelson Lang, but I just took a new box of saltines off the shelf, told Mack to put it on my mom's charge, and walked out. So much for fair-weather friends!

Good thing, most folk around here aren't like Alice. At least a dozen people stopped me in town to tell me how they're with Aunt Rachel one hundred percent, going on about how she's always been so lovely and even-tempered and good-natured ever since she was a little girl.

I heard Mom on the phone with Aunt Julie. She was telling her how worried she was for a while there that Aunt Rachel might miscarry or something, if the cops had arrested her. What's more, if the police did haul her off to jail, dragging her into some awful interrogation room, and started pumping her, trying to break her down until she couldn't stand it anymore, she might crack under the pressure and sign a trumped-up confession. She'd lose the baby, go to jail for a crime she didn't commit . . . It would be tragic. I see stories like that on television all the time. It's one thing on TV where there's always some great-looking detective or lawyer who saves the heroine in the nick of time, but this is real life!

It'd be so cruel and awful if Aunt Rachel went to jail and lost that poor little baby. My niece or nephew. Or both. Who knows? It could be twins. I'd be totally heartbroken if anything happened to those babies. This becoming an aunt is serious business. I've got to look out for Aunt Rachel.

She seems to be doing okay, though. Even Mom says she's very impressed with how well Aunt Rachel is handling all this. Sometimes, Grandpa Leo says, it takes a crisis to show your real mettle. I'm not exactly sure what he means by that, but I know he's proud of Aunt Rachel.

The sixty-four-thousand-dollar question is, who did kill Nelson? And could Aunt Rachel be in danger? What if she knows something only she doesn't know she knows it, but the killer knows she knows it and doesn't know she doesn't know it . . . ?

March 30

I suppose I'm just a naturally suspicious person, but not a week after the cops are out here questioning Aunt Rachel, a stranger's come to town. Not just to town, but right to WPIT. Applying for the job as a sales rep. Aunt Rachel's interviewing him for the position this afternoon.

I think this is a little too coincidental. This guy doesn't look like a sales rep to me. What if he's a hit man? What if he's the very man who murdered Nelson? And now he's come out here to get Aunt Rachel. I pointed this out to my mom, figuring she, of all people, would be suspicious of this new guy. But she gave me one of her looks that she always gives me when she thinks I'm letting my imagination run away with itself. "He's got excellent references, Skye," she tells me in her "I'm trying to be patient with you, dear" voice. She even added that Sid Loft, WPIT's program director, checked him out thoroughly and he's exactly who he says he is. Mom thinks this new guy could be a real asset to the station.

Not that she isn't concerned about him, but not for the reasons I am. She's just worried that Aunt Rachel and this Delaney Parker are going to fall for each other. Let's face it, men are always falling for Aunt Rachel. Right now, what with her being pregnant and this awful murder business hanging over her head, she's pretty vulnerable—which is how Mom put it to Grandpa Leo

the other night when they thought I was out of ear-
shot. I happen to be blessed with excellent hearing. If
only my teeth were half as good as my hearing. Mom
says they will be, once these damn braces come off next
year; but that's not important now.

I'm sure that Aunt Rachel is going to hire Delaney
Parker. And I'm willing to bet my Poli Sci autographed
picture that she does fall for him. Delaney Parker's su-
per good-looking—kind of a cross between Mel Gib-
son and Clint Black. I'm not a big fan of country music,
but I make an exception where Clint Black is concerned. I'd make an exception for Delaney Parker, too,
if I could be absolutely convinced he wasn't out to get
Aunt Rachel. I'm planning to keep a close watch on
him.

2

RACHEL STARED DOWN AT Delaney Parker's résumé for
several minutes as he sat patiently across from her. She
wasn't really reading it; she was simply waiting for the
wave of morning sickness to pass. Why did they call it
"morning" sickness if it hit you, without warning, any
time of the day or night?

"Is there something about my résumé that troubles
you, Miss Hart?" Delaney asked finally, not failing to
note that the woman who'd looked so tan in her photo,
was, in person, looking a little green around the gills.

Rachel shifted her gaze to him, but the movement
made her even more queasy. "Would you . . . excuse
me . . . for . . . ?" She wasn't able to finish the sentence
as she dashed out of her tiny office and made a beeline
for the bathroom.

Exiting a couple of minutes later, she was embarrassed to find her new employee-to-be out in the hall
waiting for her. He looked concerned.

"I'm sorry," she muttered, not able to look him in the
eye. She smoothed down her white silk blouse and
stuck her hands in her gray wool slacks pockets.

"Something you ate?" Delaney asked innocently. He
couldn't very well give away that he knew she was
pregnant and that might be the cause of her mad dash
to the bathroom.

"No," she said ruefully. "Not something I ate."

"Would you rather put this off till tomorrow, Miss Hart?" He hesitated. "Or if there's something I can do for you, get you..." He spread out his hands, palms up, as if at a loss as to how he might help her. The first rule of undercover work: Win the trust of the investigatee. Show your willingness—hell, eagerness—to offer assistance. If his assessment of his suspect was right, she looked to be a woman in serious need of help.

Rachel wavered for a moment. Wouldn't it be nice to have some warm, kind, not to mention extremely attractive man to lean on—just until the queasiness passed? Only, something told her it wouldn't pass for a long while, and she was determined not to fall into that old trap. She was determined to start standing on her own two feet.

Forcing a look of composure, she said, "No. I'm feeling better now."

"I'm glad to hear it."

Rachel nodded, thinking to herself that she really wanted to end this interview and simply offer him the job. He was certainly eminently qualified. He probably ought to be doing *her* job. She certainly didn't know what she was doing. Even though Morey had spent practically the whole week breaking her in. The problem was, she'd had to go down to the Chicken Coop for her education in TV sales management because Morey couldn't get away from the restaurant, and the smell of grease and barbecue sauce made her so sick it was hard to concentrate.

She was aware of Delaney Parker's waiting to continue the interview, and was about to offer him the job right on the spot, when she reminded herself that she was done taking people—especially men—at face value. She did have to admit he had a very impressive résumé, but maybe it was *too* impressive? Why would a man with the background and experience Delaney Parker had, want a job with a small-town station like WPIT? Why would someone who'd worked in places like Omaha and St. Louis, want to settle for a job in a place like Pittsville? Was he running away from something? Or someone? A man with a broken heart?

There she was, letting herself get all soft and romantic again. More than likely, if there'd been any hearts broken, they probably belonged to the women Delaney Parker had dumped. Yes, he certainly impressed her as more the dumper type than the dumpee.

She gave him a wary look. There were a lot of things about Delaney Parker she needed to know before she went and handed him a job. Especially a job that would put them in close working proximity.

"If you'd like to come back into my office . . ."

"Are you sure you wouldn't rather conduct the interview outside? It's a beautiful day, surprisingly warm for this time of year, and the fresh air might be good for both of us," Delaney suggested. The truth was, he was finding that small office confining, himself. Being in such close quarters with a murder suspect did that to him sometimes. It didn't help matters any when they were attractive—in this case, very attractive. And pregnant. He'd never had to arrest a pregnant woman for murder before. He thought ruefully that there were some firsts he could live without.

Rachel observed him more closely. His remark about the fresh air doing them both good struck her as curious. "Aren't you feeling well?"

He smiled, conveying a touch of vulnerability. Women were always suckers for a hint of vulnerability in men. "I'm a little nervous."

Rachel didn't hide her surprise. "You conceal it very well."

His smile deepened. He laid it on thick, with captivating charm. "I could dash into the bathroom."

She laughed, finding him appealing despite herself. "Okay, I'll get my jacket and we can walk around the green."

Delaney followed Rachel back into her office, helping her on with her flannel-lined red wool blazer. She lifted her hair out from under her collar, letting it fall over her shoulders, a motion that Delaney found disquietingly sensual. Her auburn curls blended very nicely with the red jacket. He noted that she looked particularly good in red, then realized, much to his consternation, that he'd have been hard put to come up with a color she wouldn't look good in. Well, maybe not prison stripes!

Getting out of the building required walking right by the studio, which could be seen through a large glass window cut into the corridor. Meg Cromwell was cooking up a storm at the stove that was built into the anchor's long desk. When not in use for Meg's prep time and for the cooking show itself, a piece of the desk top fit over it. A versatile space—necessary when you had only one small studio from which to broadcast.

Rachel checked her watch. "Cooking with Cromwell" was due to air in fifteen minutes.

Meg caught their eye as they were walking by and waved them in. Rachel gave a low groan, but it was loud enough for Delaney to hear.

"What's wrong?" he asked.

"One of Meg's taste tests. I don't think my stomach's up for it," Rachel said weakly. Even under the best of circumstances, Rachel wasn't a fan of Meg Cromwell's "inventive" concoctions.

Meg was already hurrying out of the studio, waylaying them in the corridor before they could make a quick getaway.

"You look so pale, Rachel," Meg exclaimed.

"She's a little under the weather," Delaney said. "We were just about to go—"

Meg shot out her hand. "You must be the new sales rep everyone in town's talking about."

Delaney grinned. "Miss Hart hasn't hired me yet."

"No," Rachel said awkwardly. "We're— That is, I'm . . . still interviewing Mr. Parker."

"What is it people are saying about me?" Delaney asked, a faint edge of concern in his voice. He wasn't worried about his cover getting blown, but it made him uneasy to stand out in a crowd. Unfortunately, in a town with a population of under two thousand, it was pretty difficult to be a new arrival and not get noticed.

Meg waved her hands about. "Oh, you know how it is when a new fellow comes to town. A nice-looking, single fellow." She had the good grace to blush.

Rachel felt a little color come back to her face, too. She certainly hoped Delaney Parker didn't think that she was going to hire him because he was handsome and unattached.

Delaney smiled, but he wasn't exactly thrilled about being the potential bait for the single women of Pittsville. He had his job cut out for him as it was, without a bunch of Pittsville's old maids angling to reel him in.

"Spare a minute and come taste my beef-and-lentil soup that I'm going to be doing on the show today," Meg said. "Rachel, it'll do you a world of good. You don't want to let yourself get run-down now, of all times."

The color quickly evaporated from Rachel's face. Just the thought of Meg's soup—never mind the smell, much less the taste—was enough to trigger another run to the bathroom. And then there was the little matter of Rachel not wanting her prospective employee to learn about her pregnancy in this offhand way.

Delaney saved the day. And her stomach. "Why don't you put some aside for us to try later?" he suggested warmly. "I'm sure you can understand that I'm eager to get on with this job interview." He flashed Meg Cromwell a fourteen-karat-gold smile.

As they headed out the door, Rachel looked up at Delaney. "You handled that very well. Only now, if you do get the job, you might be sorry. Meg's very likely to make up daily care packages for you."

"If she's really that bad a cook, why is she the star of your cooking show?" he asked, holding the door open for her.

"She's got a lot of personality. And some folks actually like her food. She's got a lot of fans here in Pittsville who never miss her show. I guess it's all a matter of individual taste."

Their eyes met for an uneasy moment as they thought about their own individual preferences—and not when it came to food. They both looked away at the same time.

Rachel was beginning to regret having agreed to tackle this job as sales manager at WPIT, much less interview this man to be her sales rep. Didn't she have enough to grapple with, what with being pregnant and having the man whom she had once thought she loved turn out to be a mobster, and then, as if that weren't bad enough, go and get himself killed?

"I'm not too bad in the kitchen," Delaney remarked to break the awkward silence as they stepped outside. "How about you?"

Rachel blanched. "In the kitchen?" She flashed on the photo the New York detective had shown her of Nelson lying facedown in the kitchen they'd once shared on Central Park West. She started to feel sick again.

Delaney was watching her closely. "Cooking. I'm a pretty good cook."

"Oh," Rachel muttered, gulping in some fresh air. "I don't cook much. I never was very good in the kitchen."

Delaney shot her a look as they headed for the green, which was a block-long square of grass in the center of town, diagonally across from the white-shingled two-story house that had been converted into WPIT eight years ago. The moist, leafy smell of spring was in the air. Little green sprigs were starting to sprout on the tree branches. Several people nodded and waved to them as they made their way across the street.

"Pretty little town you've got here, Miss Hart," Delaney remarked. To his surprise, Pittsville—despite its name—had turned out to be as Kelso had advertised: "a quaint little touch of Americana." The houses and shops bordering the green were very much in the style of WPIT's homey, old-fashioned quarters. Nothing lavish, but well-kept and pristine, many of the frame and shingled buildings dated back one hundred years or more. The bed-and-breakfast he was staying at, which was just off the green, had been built in 1805. Even the few newer homes in the area had been constructed in a traditional style so they didn't stick out like sore thumbs. The setting, too, was tranquil and picturesque; the whole town was dotted with stately trees and ringed with hills, beyond which rose the Berkshire Mountains.

"Pittsville must be quite a contrast from Omaha," Rachel said. Delaney Parker's résumé had indicated his last job had been as a TV sales rep for WROS in Omaha for the past two years.

Delaney had actually spent all of two days in Omaha, just before arriving in Pittsville—a fast weekend jaunt to get the lay of the land just in case he was asked any questions about the city. He'd actually spent a good part of the last two years working undercover as a driver and, ultimately, as a confidant to a notorious drug dealer who was now, thanks in large part to his undercover work, sitting in a jail cell awaiting arraignment.

"There's something special about small-town life that you just don't get in a city," Delaney said expansively, almost meaning it. Maybe he'd been living with the grit and grime for too long. "There's a warmth and friendliness. An openness. Everyone knows you. . . ."

"And all your business," Rachel added with a wry smile.

"Is that a problem for you?" Delaney asked as casually as he could.

Rachel stopped abruptly, folding her arms across her chest. She stared up at him for several seconds, deliberating. "Look, if you do end up staying here, you'll find out soon enough. And if you aren't going to stay here, it doesn't matter anyway if you do know. I'm pregnant. The father of my baby is . . . dead. I've been the sales manager at WPIT for exactly one week. I'm sure you know a lot more about the business than I ever will. I was going to ask you a lot of questions because . . . well, because I'm trying to be more . . ." She stopped, searching for the right word.

"Cautious?" Delaney suggested.

"That'll do."

They started walking again, heading down a path that cut diagonally across the green, leading to a large covered bandstand in the center. During the summer, there was a concert held there every Wednesday night. Locals and tourists alike would come with lawn chairs or blankets, carting picnic baskets, and make a night of it. Rachel used to love going to those concerts when she was a kid. Maybe someday she'd be taking her own child to them. There were a lot worse places than Pittsville to raise a kid. It would be nice having family around—her father, her sister, her niece.

Rachel was well aware Kate had given her this position as sales manager at the station more out of pity than anything else, but she was resolved to do the best job she could. Unlike both Kate and Julie, Rachel had never had much luck finding herself professionally. She'd flitted from career to career, never really getting absorbed in any of them. Working at the station began to feel like her last chance. After all, it wasn't just her anymore. She was going to be a mother. It was time to settle down and be more responsible. She made up her mind there and then to apply herself and learn everything there was to learn about bringing in advertising revenue.

It was no secret that WPIT wasn't exactly thriving. Rachel knew that if she could bring in some more local advertisers as well as national ones, she would win Kate's respect—and gain some much needed self-respect, as well. With all of his experience and superb recommendations in the field, there really was little doubt in Rachel's mind that Delaney Parker could be a big help to her. Still, she was determined not to offer him the job impulsively. She was going to be *cautious* for once in her life.

Delaney was aware of a shift in Rachel's mood. She was turning out to be more complex than he'd anticipated. Which didn't make him happy. Actually, he wasn't sure how he was feeling. Not a good sign. He rubbed his hands together, getting back to business. "So, what kind of questions were you going to ask me?"

"Do you believe in true love?" The question just popped out of Rachel's mouth. She'd meant to ask him why he'd want a job at a two-bit station like WPIT.

Delaney stared at her, his mouth hanging open. And he wasn't a guy to be easily surprised.

Rachel blushed scarlet. "Oh, it isn't . . . . I wasn't . . ." She stopped, sagging down onto a bench. Her hand darted into her pocketbook. "Saltines. I need some saltines," she muttered.

Delaney blinked. "Saltines?"

"Oh, here they are," she said, unwrapping the packet, then taking quick bites of first one cracker, then another, then another. "They...settle your...stomach."

Delaney stood there, staring down at her, at a loss for words.

She started coughing, the last cracker getting stuck in her throat. "Water," she said, springing up and heading for the fountain beside the bandstand. She took long gulps. When she turned around, wiping her mouth on the back of her hand, Delaney was right there behind her. She shut her eyes, willing him to disappear.

"Yes," he said, offering up a tender smile.

"Yes, what?" Rachel asked, relieved that at least her stomach was starting to settle even if her mind was out of whack.

"Yes, I believe in true love," he said. "In the *possibility* of true love." Delaney figured that was the answer she wanted to hear. And he was there to give her whatever she wanted in the hopes that he'd get what he needed in the end. A conviction. Or proof positive that she was innocent. That would be nice, since he didn't feature having to put a beautiful, pregnant woman behind bars. Hell, if he could buy the possibility of true love maybe he could buy that Rachel Hart didn't stab her lover in the back.

"Well, you're wrong," Rachel retorted. "Wrong, wrong, wrong."

Oops. Now what? Delaney thought. "Does this mean you won't hire me? I mean, I've not gotten other jobs in my life, but I don't think it was ever for believing in the possibility of true love. With," he hastened to add in an attempt at damage control, "a strong emphasis on *possibility.*"

"It's a trap," Rachel said firmly. "Love is a trap, Mr. Parker."

"A trap?"

"No," she corrected herself. "An illusion."

Delaney rubbed his jaw. "An illusion. Well . . ."

"Which, in reality, turns out to be a delusion. We delude ourselves, Mr. Parker. True love. There is no truth to it at all."

Delaney cocked a thick eyebrow. "There isn't?"

"No." Rachel sat down on the steps of the bandstand. "We meet someone—someone who seems sweet, tender, understanding, gentle, giving—only in the end he turns out to be absolutely nothing like the way he seemed. And do you know why, Mr. Parker?"

Delaney wrinkled his brow. To say this interview was not going according to any plan he'd envisioned was a definite understatement. Still, it was leading to some potentially hot stuff.

"I think I have a good guess," he said quietly. "I think some people are very skilled at deception. They make you think they're one thing when they're really something else altogether, because it's to their advantage." Speaking as one who knew. Was that a twinge of guilt he was feeling? Naw. Just indigestion. Maybe he needed a few of those saltine crackers himself.

Conscience or no, Rachel was beaming up at him like he'd gotten the final word right in the spelling bee. "Exactly, Mr. Parker." She hesitated. "Can I call you Delaney?"

He sat down on the steps beside her. "Sure. Sure you can."

She turned and looked at him. "Why do you really want this job, Delaney?"

He forced himself to meet her level gaze. "I guess I've always been a small cog in a big wheel, and this is my chance to be—"

"A big cog in a very small wheel?" Rachel finished for him.

He smiled. "WPIT has a lot of potential."

She liked his enthusiasm.

"Besides," he added, "I've always wanted to settle in the Berkshires, ever since I came here to camp when I was a kid."

"What camp?"

"Singing Brook. Over in Camfield. I believe it was sold about ten years ago and it's a shopping mall now." At least that was what his research assistant had in her report. "Real pity. I really loved that place. The great outdoors, all that fresh mountain air. Not to brag or anything, but I won a blue ribbon in archery." He always did try to hit his mark. Bull's-eye.

"Singing Brook? That was a camp for..." Rachel hesitated.

"For poor city kids who didn't know one end of a fishing rod from the other," Delaney said with just a touch of a smile.

In truth, he'd never been to Singing Brook. Never been to the Berkshires before in his life. He had, however, attended a camp similar to Singing Brook in Pennsylvania when he was a poor street kid growing up in Brooklyn. In doing undercover work, Delaney had found it was always smart to stick as close to the truth as possible.

"And do you know which end is up now?" Rachel asked with real interest in her voice. It would be good if one of them did.

Delaney felt his stomach start to act up again. "Sometimes I wonder," he admitted.

"I know what you mean," Rachel said, looking off into the distance. With all that had happened, she wasn't sure if she would ever know which end was up ever again.

"When is your baby due?" Delaney asked quietly.

"November." She placed her hand on her stomach, willing it to start to swell. "A little more than six months from now."

"November. That's a nice time to have a baby," Delaney muttered. If she wasn't sitting in a jail cell at the time. He was liking this assignment less and less. Or was it that he was liking his suspect more and more? Not a good situation either way.

"Do you have any children, Delaney?" Rachel asked.

"Children?" Delaney's brow furrowed. "No. No, I'm not married."

"Neither am I," Rachel stated matter-of-factly.

That's it, Delaney. Don't just stick your foot in your mouth, stick it down your throat. "Look, I'm . . . sorry. Really. I . . ."

Rachel patted his arm. "Don't feel bad, Delaney. It could be a lot worse. I could have married the baby's father." She looked away.

Delaney had to look surprised. He wasn't supposed to know about the father of Rachel's baby. "You two didn't . . . get along?" *Easy, Delaney. Don't force it.*

"The baby's father—my former fiancé—was Nelson Lang."

Rachel waited for a reaction from Delaney, but he kept a blank expression. "Should I know him?"

"You should if you read the papers or watch the news on television," Rachel said, surprised that Nelson's name didn't even ring a bell with him.

Delaney furrowed his brow dramatically. "Wait a minute. Nelson Lang. Nelson Lang. Yeah, I do remember seeing something—" He stopped, letting the play of emotions reveal themselves on his face.

Rachel nodded. It was obvious Delaney remembered plenty now. "I still can't believe someone murdered him," Rachel said in a muted voice. "I suppose, though, when you live the sort of life Nelson lived— awful things can happen to you." She sighed wearily. "I'm sorry he's dead, but I can't honestly say I miss him or even feel . . . all that bad."

Slowly, Delaney turned to her. Was he looking into the face of a murderer? He knew from experience that murderers came in every shape, size and color. Plenty of them didn't look like killers. Not too many of them, though, looked as good as Rachel Hart. Which didn't prove anything except that this assignment would be a lot easier if his suspect looked like Whistler's mother, and acted like a first-class bitch instead of being so damn appealing and ingenuous.

"He was stabbed," she went on, a melancholy undercurrent in her voice. "It happened just after I left him."

"You left him?"

She blinked, shaking off the daze that was starting to sink in. It was all still so hard to believe.

"I thought he was a bird-watcher."

Delaney was sure he couldn't have heard her right. "Excuse me?"

She shrugged. "It doesn't matter now. Yes. I left him. What other choice did I have?" The question was clearly rhetorical, but Delaney could have given her some answers. Like maybe she'd have had more choices if she hadn't stabbed him to death. He warned himself not to start jumping to conclusions. The reason he was so good at what he did was that he always managed to keep an open mind. Allowed him to let more info filter in.

Delaney was itching to get deeper into this conversation, but he bided his time. He hadn't expected her to talk so openly about Lang so soon and he didn't want to get greedy. *Give her time. Give her room. Give her a chance to talk about it in her own way, at her own pace.*

"There's one thing, Delaney, that I need to know before I can offer you this job."

Her voice pulled him from his thoughts. "Yes?"

She gave him a long, level look. "I need to know that I can trust you. That there aren't going to be any... surprises down the road."

What could he say to her? How could he answer her? Sometimes, this business he was in really sucked. Meanwhile she was waiting—for reassurance, from the look in her eyes.

"Trust is a two-way street, Rachel. It takes time and effort. I'm willing to put in both if you are."

Okay, he thought, it was a cop-out, but it was sort of the truth. If he wasn't exactly willing to give her the benefit of the doubt at this point, he wasn't going to try and convict her in his mind without more proof, either.

As he looked at Rachel, waiting to see how she'd take his answer, he spotted a young girl in jeans and a sweatshirt ducking behind a nearby tree. Probably playing a game of hide-and-seek with her friends, he decided, turning his full attention back to Rachel.

She smiled tentatively. "When can you start?"

"Right now," he said, smiling back. It wasn't a smile that came easily.

April 3

Phew! That was a close call. Parker—if that's even his name—almost spotted me when I tailed him and Aunt Rachel to the green yesterday. I ducked out of sight just in the nick of time.

She hired him for the job. Big surprise. Everyone's so happy. I can't believe it. Nobody seems to think there's something fishy here but me. Mom even invited him over for dinner Saturday night. Everyone's going to be there—me and Mom, Aunt Rachel naturally, Grandpa

Leo and his girlfriend, Mellie, even Aunt Julie who flew in from DC this morning.

I went over to the Daisy Inn this afternoon after school only to discover Parker had already checked out. Daisy Osborne told me he's gone and rented the old Seymour place on Millbrook Road. I think I'll just bike out there after school tomorrow and have a look around while Parker's down at the station working.

I know some people would call it snooping, but I call it "investigating." Anyway, somebody's got to look after Aunt Rachel's best interests. I bet she's already gaga over Parker, whether she knows it or not. Everyone who meets him seems to think he's so neat. Aunt Julie met him down at the station, and after talking with him for exactly five minutes, told my mom that Aunt Rachel could do a lot worse than Parker, and Mom actually agreed, even if she was a little reluctant about it. Grandpa Leo was more enthusiastic. I think they've all decided that Aunt Rachel's baby is going to need a father. I'm a little disappointed in Aunt Julie. I thought she of all people would share my suspicions about Parker, but it's like he's cast a "charming" spell over the lot of them.

Not me, though. Personally, I think they all need to have their heads examined—one of Mom's favorite lines. I can see why, now.

3

"ARE YOU SURE YOU won't have any more lamb stew,
Delaney?" Kate asked, dipping the ladle into the large
casserole dish. For all her reservations about men in
general, she liked a man who appreciated her cooking.

Delaney patted his lean, flat stomach. "Two help-
ings are all I can manage, thanks. I couldn't eat another bite, but it was delicious. Best food I've had since
I've been here in Pittsville. Nothing like a home-cooked
meal."

"Did you have a lot of home-cooked meals out in
Omaha?" Skye asked bluntly, ignoring both her mother's and her two aunts' disapproving looks.

"Not many," Delaney said to the twelve-year-old
who was the spitting image in miniature of her attractive mother. He was convinced at this point that Skye
was the girl he'd seen dart behind a tree last week when
he and Rachel were on the bandstand at the green. She'd
been spying on them—or, more to the point, on him.
And she hadn't stopped there. There were those bicy-
cle-tire tracks he'd spotted on the dirt path leading to
his cottage the next afternoon when he returned home
from his first day "on the job." A neighbor of his down
the road mentioned seeing Skye ride by that day and
since the road ended at his property, there was little
doubt as to her destination. She'd been snooping

around inside his place, which had been easy enough to get into since the Realtor was still trying to dig up the keys to the property. It seemed no one in Pittsville locked their doors.

From the look of it, Skye had done a neat but thorough job of going through his small, one-bedroom cottage. Papers on his living room desk had been moved slightly, clothes in his bureau drawers had been shifted. Even his laundry bag had been searched—the socks he'd thrown on top of the pile that morning having made their way down to the middle. He had to hand it to the kid, though. If he hadn't been a pro, he might not have noticed anything amiss. The question was, what was she looking for? And why was she so suspicious of him, whereas everyone else in the family—especially Rachel—seemed to have bought his cover so completely?

"Rachel's the one who should eat more stew," Mellie Oberchon declared, nudging her wire-rimmed glasses up higher on the bridge of her nose. "She's eating for two now."

Grandpa Leo, a handsome, robust man in his early seventies, squeezed Mellie's veined hand affectionately. Mellie was a petite woman with snow-white hair worn in a halo of soft curls around her heart-shaped face. Though well into her sixties, she would still have to be described as "cute." She and Leo had been dating—or, as they both called it, "courting"—for nearly five months now. The Hart girls were all fond of Mellie, who'd come back to Pittsville nearly a year ago after her husband had died, and had moved in with her sister.

The sister was the problem. Agnes Pilcher was Kate's ex-mother-in-law. Even before Kate and Arnie Pilcher divorced, Kate's relationship with Agnes hadn't been particularly convivial. Since the divorce, and especially since Kate ended up with WPIT in the divorce settlement, the two women had been openly at odds, Agnes disapproving of how Kate was running the station, and believing that she should be the one in charge. There wasn't much about Kate, for that matter, that Agnes did approve of. Nor was she particularly enamored of the rest of the Hart family. Especially Leo Hart, whom she herself had been courted by nearly fifty years back. That her younger sister was now dating Leo only added insult to injury as far as Agnes was concerned.

With a bit more coaxing from Mellie, who was something of a mother hen, Rachel agreed to another scoop of stew. Actually, this was the first time in weeks that she'd had any appetite to speak of. Maybe her morning sickness was finally beginning to pass. Or it could be that she was feeling more settled now and less anxious about—everything.

Rachel's eyes fell on Delaney who was sitting directly across from her at the big, oval oak table in Kate's dining room. She wondered if he was in any way responsible for her new calm. He certainly seemed to have a soothing effect on her. For one thing, he was so confident and self-assured about his work. Only there a week and he'd already made several contacts with some of the major ad agencies in Manhattan, scheduling a meeting with one of the top people at DMG&G for the following Monday. In his five years on the job, Morey

Lewis had never made so much as an inroad into an agency of the caliber of DMG&G. Clearly, Delaney Parker's background, past experience, and connections gave him an enormous advantage. However, it wasn't only his take-charge manner on the job that made Rachel feel that hiring him had been the smartest thing she'd done in a long time; it was also his warm, sympathetic and caring manner toward her. He inspired confidence, encouraged her to believe she could tackle anything. There certainly was plenty ahead to tackle.

Delaney had plenty to tackle, too. Over the past week, he'd gotten exactly nowhere with Rachel as far as his investigation into the murder of Nelson Lang went. Not wanting to broach the topic of the mobster himself at this point, he kept waiting for Rachel to give him an opening, but she never once mentioned Lang's name all week. All they'd talked about since he'd started work that Monday had been the business of selling TV time to sponsors. As far as her mood went, she appeared upbeat, enthusiastic, and eager to get on with her life. If she had murdered her lover, she certainly wasn't wearing a guilty conscience on her sleeve. Either she was a consummate actress, a sociopath, or . . . she hadn't done it.

Delaney's frustration was mounting. Word from New York was that neither Mendez nor Kelso had been making any better progress in their investigations into the Lang slaying. A number of people who'd been affiliated with the mobster had been brought in for questioning, but while most of them had motive and means, they also had solid alibis, thus eliminating the crucial *opportunity*. Rachel Hart, having all three, was still number one on both Kelso's and Mendez's suspect list, and pressure was being brought to bear from the DA's office to pin the murder on someone soon.

Mendez had made it clear to Delaney that he expected him to bring in some hard evidence on Rachel. Easier said than done. Especially as he couldn't seem to completely dismiss the glimmer of hope that maybe they were all barking up the wrong tree. There was still Suzanne, the mystery woman who'd written Lang that love letter. What if it turned out that she, not Rachel, was *the woman scorned*? Suzanne could have shown up that night for a showdown with Lang; he could have dumped her; she could have picked up that kitchen knife....

Pure conjecture, and Delaney knew it. Meanwhile, they didn't even know her last name. Both the cops and the FBI were trying to track her down. No luck so far.

Delaney could feel Rachel's eyes on him. He looked up from his plate and gave her a faint smile, struck by just how much he'd come to hope over this past week that she wasn't guilty. He liked her; liked her whole family. Nice, wholesome, decent people. He was beginning to think this was the worst undercover assignment he'd ever had the misfortune to land. Even if it turned out Rachel was guilty, he didn't particularly relish the thought of being the one to have to bring her in. He felt his throat start to tighten, an edginess sneaking in under his skin. Never fall in *like* with a suspect, he told himself wryly, not wanting to question if what he was beginning to feel for Rachel Hart was more than *like*.

Rachel saw the shift of emotions play out on Delaney's face and she worried that he might have read too much into her smile. She certainly didn't want him to think she was coming on to him in any way. She liked Delaney, admired him, respected him, but that was all it was. That was all she wanted there to be. She focused on her food.

"This stew is good, Kate. You'll have to give me the recipe," she muttered as she brought a forkful to her mouth.

Kate merely smiled. Was her little sister actually turning *domestic?*

Julie Hart, who'd been surprisingly quiet throughout most of the dinner, abruptly leveled her gaze on Rachel, impatience finally getting the better of her. No big surprise. It usually did.

"I just don't get it," she declared, resting both palms on the cloth-covered table.

All eyes fell on Julie. Skye could feel the tension suddenly fill the room like a blast of chilly air on a hot summer night. At last, the end of all the boring chitchat, she thought. Leave it to her Aunt Julie to stir things up.

"What don't you get?" Rachel asked warily. Ever since her arrival Julie had been quizzing her about Nelson's murder. The last thing Rachel wanted was for her ex-lover's death to be the topic of conversation at the dinner table. Especially with Delaney there.

"I'll tell you what I don't get. I don't get why Lang's murder is getting so little media attention," Julie said, needing no prodding.

Rachel sighed. It was too much to expect that her sister would show some *discretion*. It wasn't Julie's style. Rachel flashed her gaze on Delaney.

Delaney played it cool, on the one hand not wanting to show too much interest, on the other not wanting his presence to inhibit the conversation in any way. He didn't have to worry. Julie Hart wasn't the type to be easily inhibited.

Julie's eyes remained fixed on Rachel. "The cops come here, ask you a few questions, and then—that's it?"

"I told them everything I knew," Rachel said in a low voice, trying to concentrate on her stew, but finding she'd lost her appetite.

Mellie turned to Leo. "My daughter, Frannie, lived with a young man for a brief time and it didn't work out, either."

"You mean he got murdered, too?" Skye piped in, incredulous.

"Oh dear, no," Mellie said, aghast. "He was just so untidy. Never picked up his things. Why, it drove Frannie to distraction. She's an exceptionally neat person. I don't know where she got it from. Not that I'm messy by any means, but my husband, George, may he rest in peace, never, in our thirty-seven years together, remembered to put his dirty socks in the hamper, and it never did particularly bother me."

Julie, bent on her own course of discussion, ignored Mellie's scatological remark. "I tried to do some digging into the investigation before I got here and it's like there's a conspiracy of silence going on. Who else have the cops questioned? Do they have any suspects? And what about the FBI? I'd bet my bottom dollar they're more than a little interested in Lang's mob connections, but I can't get a word out of anyone in DC. It's very suspicious."

"Really, Julie," Kate said sharply. "I don't think this is the time or place...."

Julie shrugged. "What are we supposed to do? Ignore it? Not mention that the man Rachel was living with was murdered? That he turned out to be a big shot in the mob? That, for all we know, Rachel is still under suspicion?"

Delaney's gaze shot to Rachel. She had gone very white and still.

Grandpa Leo gave Julie a chastising look, but Rachel saw there was no escaping this.

"Julie's right," she admitted. "It is odd. I keep trying to put the whole sad, awful business out of my mind, but sometimes I wake up in the middle of the night and wonder why the police didn't just come here and arrest me." She omitted describing the feelings of panic and fear that accompanied those thoughts.

"They had no proof, that's why," Skye interjected. "It's all circumstantial evidence. Isn't that right, Aunt Julie?"

Julie beamed at her niece. "You are going to make an ace journalist one of these days, Skye. You're absolutely right. They need some hard evidence."

"Which, of course, since Aunt Rachel is totally innocent, there isn't any," Skye declared fiercely.

"There's no question about that," Leo said firmly. "It'll all get settled soon enough."

"Like I always say, things work out as they should in the end," Mellie said, smiling at Rachel. "Look at Frannie. She found Mike—the man's neat as a pin—and they've been happily married for seven years now."

Julie rolled her eyes. She was fond of her father's girlfriend, but there was no denying the woman was a little ditsy. "Rachel, if you could give me any leads to go on, there's a chance, with my connections, that I could dig something up."

"I could help," Skye said, casting a quick glance at Delaney, then returning her gaze to her aunt. "I might even have a few ideas of my own."

Kate rose and started clearing the table. "Why don't we have coffee and dessert in the living room?" She was hoping a change of scene would help bring about a change in the conversation.

Rachel got up, feeling a little queasy. So much for the end of her morning sickness. "I'm just going to step out on the porch for a few minutes. To get some fresh air."

Delaney rose, too. "I could use a bit of fresh air myself. Mind if I join you, Rachel?"

She managed a weak smile. "No. Of course not."

Mellie smiled at Leo as the pair left the dining room. "I wouldn't be a bit surprised if those two were keen on each other," she murmured.

Kate, meanwhile, gave Julie an irritated look. "Now see what you've done. You've gone and got Rachel all worked up again."

Julie smoothed back her blond hair, which she wore in a short, stylish cut currently in vogue among the top women television newscasters. Even dressed in jeans and a pullover, she retained an air of cool sophistication. She eyed her older sister defiantly. "You can't hide this nasty business under a rug, Kate. Rachel said as much herself. Something's going on and I'm not at all convinced Rachel's home free. The cops could be quietly going around building a case against her. We've got to be prepared—"

"The only thing we need to prepare for is getting the coffee and dessert out," Kate said, cutting her off. "Rachel had nothing to do with Nelson Lang's murder. If she was under suspicion still, we'd know about it, and we'd deal with it. But she's in the clear and I'm sure the police have any number of disreputable creeps on their list of suspects. You're always reading in the paper about—"

"Exactly," Julie interrupted. "You're always reading about these gangster killings in the papers. Only this time you aren't. Doesn't that make you wonder?"

"I'll tell you what makes me wonder," Kate said, briskly cleaning off the dinner plates as she stacked them. "Your total lack of insensitivity. Didn't you see how upset Rachel got when you brought up Lang's name? And in front of a practical stranger, no less."

"He's strange, all right," Skye muttered.

"I think Mr. Parker's a delightful man," Mellie said.

"Come on, Kate," Julie protested. "I'm sure Delaney's heard gossip galore in town about Rachel and Nelson. He must know it's on all our minds."

"That doesn't mean it should be dinner conversation," Kate countered.

"Girls, girls," Leo interjected in. "Let's not fight now."

"I just don't want Rachel getting upset," Kate said. "Especially now. The first trimester of a pregnancy can be tricky. Too much stress . . ."

"Rachel knows I'm one hundred percent behind her," Julie said. "Besides, she herself admitted that she's scared. I just don't think it's healthy for the rest of us to deny that she might still be under investigation. . . ."

Skye was trying to slip unobtrusively out of the room, hoping to do a little eavesdropping on the pair out on the porch, when her mother caught sight of her. "Where are you off to, young lady?"

Skye came to an abrupt halt. "Who, me? I was just . . . I thought I'd go outside and check on the tires on my bike. They might need air."

Mellie smiled mischievously at Skye. "I remember when I was just about your age and got my first crush on an older man."

Skye's eyes widened. "What?"

Mellie blushed. "It was your grandfather, actually. I remember wanting to sneak outside when he and Aggie were sitting together on the porch and just watch him. He was so handsome. He still is."

Leo bussed Mellie's cheek. "You always say the sweetest things."

Everyone smiled except Skye, whose eyes were riveted in shock on Mellie. "You don't think . . . that I . . . that me and Parker . . . that I have a crush on Delaney Parker . . . ?"

"Oh, I don't think that's it," Kate said offhandedly. "Skye's convinced there's something suspicious about him. She's got all kinds of wild theories."

Julie focused in on her niece. "Really," she mused. "What kinds of theories, Skye?"

"Don't get her started," Kate said. "Skye, forget about your *bike* and go into the kitchen and put on the coffee. Julie, you help me with these dishes. Mellie, why don't you and Dad go into the living room and relax? Why don't we *all* just relax?" Her gaze zeroed in on Julie. "And no more talk about Nelson Lang tonight."

"I'M NOT SURE IF I EVER was really in love with Nelson," Rachel confessed. She was sitting beside Delaney on the forest green Adirondack bench on the porch that ran the length of the front of Kate's house and overlooked a quiet street dotted with similar-vintage frame houses and tidy front lawns. It was a warm night, the stillness punctuated by the sound of crickets and the gentle rustling of leaves.

"Naturally, I thought I was in love with him at the time. Or at least with the fictitious character he created and which I bought into," Rachel hastened to add. "Otherwise, I would never have agreed to move in with him. Nelson was the first man I ever lived with."

"Was that his idea?" Delaney asked in what he hoped was a casual tone.

"*He* asked *me*, naturally. I'm not the pushy type."

Delaney smiled. No, a woman who looked like Rachel wouldn't have to "push."

"We were always together. We were talking about getting married. He thought living together first made sense. And I thought it did, too." She looked to Delaney for confirmation.

"Oh . . . right."

"You disapprove?"

"Me? No."

"Have you ever lived with a woman, Delaney?"

Delaney frowned. He was much better at asking the questions than answering them. Especially when it came to his private life. "Well . . . I guess. For a brief time. Here and there." *Brief* was the operative word. Only lately had he begun toying seriously with the idea of settling down, having a family, creating roots.

Rachel smiled.

Her smile made him uncomfortable. "What?"

"I figured you for a real ladies' man. A regular heart-breaker."

Delaney's eyes narrowed. "You did?"

"You're a very good-looking man, Delaney. Speaking purely objectively." She tried to sound objective, even if that wasn't how she was feeling.

"Meaning not subjectively?"

"No. That is, yes. I mean . . ."

"I'm not your type."

"No. No, I wouldn't say that."

A smile played on his lips. "Then you're saying I *am* your type."

Rachel blushed. "No. I wouldn't say that, either."

"What would you say?" he prodded, enjoying this bit of flirtatious banter more than he knew he should.

Rachel had worked herself into a corner. The truth was, Delaney Parker was her type. Just the type she was looking for, as a matter of fact. Only the fact of the matter was that she had vowed to stop looking. Her judgment to date hadn't exactly won her any prizes—except maybe the booby prize.

She absently smoothed back some wayward curls from her face. "Weren't we talking about my moving into Nelson's apartment?"

Delaney nodded, annoyed with himself for leaving it to Rachel to get them back on track. For a moment he'd almost forgotten why he was there.

"To be absolutely honest," she said hurriedly in her effort to shift the focus away from her growing attraction to Delaney, "Nelson's apartment was about a hundred cuts above mine. Being a research assistant didn't exactly pay me big bucks. I was living in a walk-up studio in the West Village. Nelson's place was . . . really beautiful. Right on Central Park West. Even the bathroom window overlooked the park."

"Didn't it surprise you that he . . . lived so well?" Delaney asked. It was still hard to buy that Rachel hadn't had some suspicions about Lang right from the start. Or was she merely your average gold-digger in sheep's clothing? If that was the case, why would she want to kill off the goose that laid the golden eggs? He could hear Mendez's voice like he was sitting on his shoulder. *Lang was ready to dump her for Suzanne. No more golden eggs. So she says to herself, "If I can't have him, no one will. . . ."*

"Nelson said his mother's second husband had owned the apartment," Rachel was saying. "When he died, she decided the place held too many sad memories for her and so she moved down to Boca Raton and let Nelson move in. . . ." She shrugged. "It made sense."

Delaney nodded. Yeah, it made sense. Especially if you thought you were in love and you wanted things to make sense. Only now, Rachel was saying, maybe she wasn't in love. Maybe none of it made any sense. Except that she had motives galore for doing Lang in.

He wondered if any part of Lang's story held even a filament of truth. If there was a mother in Boca, he'd get word to Mendez to have her questioned. Did she and her son get along? Where was she the night Lang was stabbed? It certainly wouldn't be the first time someone was murdered by a member of their family. Of course, Rachel was almost family. She and Lang had been engaged. Try as he might to get on a new path, it seemed invariably to circle back to Rachel.

"Did you ever meet his mother?" Delaney asked, hoping for a description.

"No, but Nelson did call her at least once a week."

"A faithful son. How touching," Delaney said sardonically. "So you spoke to her on the phone."

Rachel grew silent. Delaney realized he was pushing awfully hard. Was she getting suspicious about him asking so many questions about her life with Lang?

"Sorry," he said. "Why don't we talk about something else?"

Rachel wasn't listening. She was deep in thought. "I never did speak to her," she said. "I wanted to, but . . ." She let the sentence go.

Delaney picked it up. It could be important. "But what?"

Rachel sighed. "Nelson never invited me to speak to her. Just the opposite. He usually made the calls from another room. I thought he was uncomfortable about his mother knowing we were living together. He did make her sound like a very traditional, conservative woman."

She pressed her lips together. "Now, I'm not even sure there was . . . a mother. Nelson lied to me about everything else. Why not that, too? He could have been talking to anyone." Rachel wasn't thinking just *anyone*, though. She was thinking, *Suzanne*. The woman who couldn't wait for her to be out of the picture so she could have Nelson all to herself. Then again, Rachel thought, there could have been other women, too. Why think, merely because she'd found that one letter, that Nelson didn't have a whole harem of girlfriends in various ports? He could have been talking to any one of them. With her right there in his apartment—half the time, right there in his bed.

"I was such an idiot," she muttered. "Kate and Julie are right."

"About what?"

She sighed. "I've always trusted people too quickly. Especially men." She glanced at Delaney. "Take you."

Delaney could feel the heat rise under his collar. "Me?"

"I probably shouldn't trust you any more than I trusted Nelson."

"Well . . ." What could he say?

She suddenly smiled. "I do trust you, though, Delaney. Even Kate and Julie trust you, which is quite an accomplishment."

What better compliment could an undercover cop get? So why wasn't he feeling elated?

Rachel got quiet. She idly traced a line on her pinstriped blue slacks in a gesture that wasn't in itself particularly provocative, but it nonetheless provoked a surprisingly physical response in Delaney that temporarily threw him.

Okay, he told himself, *so she turns me on a little. A little more than a little. Big surprise. She's a beautiful, sexy woman.* It would be abnormal not to experience a flash of arousal now and then. He could handle it. He was a professional.

Rachel propped her sandal-clad feet on the edge of the bench and clasped her hands around her knees. "I get the feeling you don't trust too many people yourself, Delaney."

"Me?"

"Especially women."

"Well . . ."

"I think you keep women at a safe distance. Maybe you believe in the *possibility* of true love, but I think the *actuality* of it scares you to death."

Delaney wasn't about to admit it, but Rachel was right on the mark. Oh, sure, the idea of finding the right woman appealed to him, but the fear that he might make the wrong choice had always kept him from looking all that hard. He wasn't looking now, either. But life was full of surprises.

Rachel, herself, kept surprising him. He wouldn't have figured her for a woman with great insight into men. Especially not into him. For all her charm and appeal, he had her down as naive, a little flighty and self-involved. Now, he realized he had stuck those labels on her merely because she was beautiful. And because he didn't much care for naive, flighty, self-involved women—which would have made her safe.

Rachel turned to him. "You want to know the difference between us when it comes to love, Delaney?"

He wasn't sure he wanted to know, but he nodded.

"My guess is you expect too little out of a relationship, and I keep making the mistake of expecting too much." A frown marred her lovely face. "Although I don't think it's too much to expect a man to be honest with me." Her frown deepened. "Or to be faithful."

"I think Lang must have been nuts to have cheated on you." The words just spilled from his mouth. Delaney told himself it was because of feeling guilty about his own dishonesty, but he knew it was more than that. Maybe he wished he hadn't said what he'd said, but there was no denying he believed every word of it.

"You do?" she asked, a faint smile playing on her lips.

Delaney smiled back. He was so tempted to lean down and kiss those full, provocative lips. Would it really be a crime?

Crime. That one word brought it all back. He was here with a crime suspect. What the hell was he doing? Okay, he hadn't *done* anything yet, but the thoughts he was starting to have were bad enough.

They broke eye contact at the same time, both filled with the same resolution not to let themselves get too carried away, here.

Rachel cleared her throat. "I've been meaning to tell you how pleased I am with the job you're doing at the station, Delaney." She could hear how stilted her voice sounded.

He grinned. "Does that mean I can ask for a raise?"

Rachel got flustered. "Well . . . no. I just meant—"

"Hey, I was only kidding. I may be ser̄
months, though."

Rachel observed him thoughtfully, even a
wistfully. "Something tells me you won't be here iᵢ
months."

Unfortunately, Delaney thought, chances were neither of them would be around these parts in six months.
He would be off in another corner of the country with
a new identity, a new assignment. And the way things
were going, she'd very likely be behind bars.

"Why do you think I'll be gone?" he asked.

She shrugged, not really sure why. A gut feeling.
"Somehow, I can't see you settling for very long in a
place like this, even if you think that's what you want
right now."

"What do you want right now, Rachel?"

They both knew it was a loaded question. Something was happening between them. They were both
dancing around the edge of the flame, and they knew
it. The heat was damn tempting, but they were both
scared of getting burned.

Rachel avoided Delaney's direct gaze, valiantly trying to fight off some of those romantic illusions she was
telling herself she no longer had.

"I guess what I want most," she said finally, "is for
the police to find Nelson's murderer. I don't think I'll
really be able to get on with my life until then."

"I'd like to see you be able to get on with your life,
Rachel." He meant every word. There was no getting
around it. He didn't want her to be guilty. Wanting,
however, didn't make it so. If he dug up hard evidence
against her, he'd have no choice but to take her in.

"You're a nice man, Delaney," Rachel said softly.

Tell me that again when you're sitting in court on trial for murder, he thought glumly.

"You thought Nelson was a nice man, too, once upon a time," he felt compelled to remind her.

Rachel scowled. "Yes, I did, didn't I?"

"Do you have any idea who killed Lang, Rachel?"

Delaney could see that she was taken aback by his blunt question. He thought fast. "It's just that I'm worried about you. About your safety. Whoever killed your boyfriend could come after you."

"Ex-boyfriend," she corrected. "I'd already left Nelson—even if it was only earlier that night—before he was killed. Anyway, why would Nelson's murderer come after me?"

Why, indeed, especially if she was the one who killed him? Delaney thought.

"Well, maybe he thinks you know something," he suggested. "Or thinks you saw something you weren't supposed to. Maybe he even thinks you were still in the apartment when Lang was stabbed." *Give me something, Rachel. Something to lead me down another path. I'm trying here, babe, but I need a little help.*

Rachel didn't answer right away. A dark blue sedan drove slowly past the house. She followed its movement, watched as it turned right at the corner.

"Delaney, this may sound crazy, but when I left Nelson's building that night, I had this funny feeling that someone was . . . lurking in the shadows."

Delaney's ears pricked up. He scrutinized her closely. "A feeling? Or you saw someone?"

"No. No, I didn't see anyone."

"A car, maybe?"

"There were lots of cars on the street. Why would one stand out?"

"It could have just pulled up. You might have caught the sound of an engine being shut off."

Rachel gave him a curious look. "I think you're in the wrong profession, Delaney."

Delaney cleared his throat. "I guess I've watched too many murder shows on TV. You get all kinds of ideas."

They stood side by side, shoulders only inches apart, both of them filled with more ideas than they could handle. And most of them had nothing to do with the murder of Nelson Lang.

"We'd better go inside," Rachel said finally. "Kate makes a fabulous blueberry pie. You won't want to miss it."

She started to turn away, but Delaney's hand stopped her. Her eyes shot up to his. He must have looked as surprised as she did. He hadn't meant to reach out for her. His hand had acted of its own volition. In his head he was thinking, *Right, blueberry pie sounds good*, but what he was really craving had nothing to do with baked goods.

Rachel felt Delaney's hand on her shoulder, his fingers grazing her neck. His gray-green eyes radiated an intensity she hadn't seen there before. She felt a little afraid, more than a little intrigued, and far more aroused than she knew was good for her.

"Don't you care for...blueberries?" she asked inanely, her voice unnaturally husky.

His face broke into a grin that was unexpectedly boyish and utterly disarming. "Never met a blueberry I didn't like."

She laughed softly. She stopped as he stepped closer to her. Both of his hands moved to her hips. His grin disappeared.

Rachel swallowed a breath as Delaney's hands slid up over her rib cage and he lowered his mouth to hers.

He was the first man she'd kissed since Nelson and it was like stepping into new, dangerous, unexplored territory. There was an intensity here that she'd never felt before. Not with Nelson. Not with any other man. His kiss—so hungry, so fierce, so deliciously wanton—made her forget he was her new employee; made her forget that she was a suspect in a murder; made her forget that her whole life was in chaos. In short, kissing Delaney made her forget everything but how good it felt.

They sprang apart as the screen door opened, both of them instantly breathless and disoriented.

"Pie's on the table," Mellie announced with a bright, knowing smile.

THE DARK BLUE SEDAN pulled to a stop halfway up the next street. The man behind the wheel checked to make sure no one was in sight, then got out of the car and started back toward the Hart house on foot. He cursed under his breath when he got within sight of the place and saw that the porch was now empty.

He hung around in the shadows for a few minutes, just in case there was any more activity. This job was beginning to get on his nerves. Watch, report in, and wait for further orders. It wasn't the way he liked to operate.

"AT TWO IN THE MORNING, there weren't a lot of people up and around on Central Park West, Delaney," Mendez said sardonically, not too thrilled to have been woken from a deep sleep after midnight by the jarring ring of the telephone. His wife, Gina, nudged him sharply in the ribs as she rolled over beside him. She wasn't too thrilled, either.

"She thinks she saw someone outside," Delaney persisted. "It could have been someone who'd just pulled up in a car. And that someone could have waited for her to leave and then gone up to Lang's apartment...."

"What kind of car? Make, model, license plate..."

"I don't know yet. I just think—"

"You know what I think, Delaney? The mountain air up there is getting to your brain. Or maybe it's the Hart woman's perfume."

"You're nuts," Delaney growled.

"You call me at this crazy hour of the night with absolutely nothing and call *me* nuts?"

"Okay, sure. What I'm telling you here is nothing. You've got the case all sewn up. Why bother making more work for yourself—"

"Look, you want to convince me the Hart woman's not our star suspect, give me something concrete to go on. Then you can call me any hour of the day or night. Oh, and just so you know we're not sitting on our duffs back here, about that gal who wrote Lang the love note. Her name's Suzanne English."

Delaney's hand tightened on the phone. "Yeah?"

"She lives in Philly. In a swank apartment that's in Lang's name. He's been paying the rent on it for the past two months."

"So?" Delaney asked impatiently.

"Forget it," Mendez said. "The dame's got a solid alibi. The night Lang was offed, she was stripping in a west Philly club for about two dozen ogling guys. The fellows we questioned say she wasn't half bad on the eyes. Then again, neither is the Hart gal, right?"

Delaney's features hardened. He didn't like the idea of Mendez grouping Rachel with some sleazy stripper. He didn't say anything, though, knowing Mendez would be quick to make too much of it.

"The DA's getting real impatient. The mayor's on his neck. She did it, Delaney. I know it. Kelso knows it. The DA knows it. We just need you to prove it. Have you had a chance, yet, to go through her things?"

"No, there's either someone around the house, or I can't get away from the station. I will get a chance on Monday before I drive into the city. Rachel and her sister will be at the station, and Kate's kid will be in school." There was still Julie, but she'd mentioned earlier that evening that she'd be spending Monday visiting friends.

"Good," Mendez said enthusiastically. "Now, if you can dig up something useful, maybe we'll be able to wrap this up and make everyone happy."

Not everyone, Delaney thought, as the phone clicked off. Wearily, he dropped the receiver in the cradle and stretched out in bed, both arms folded under his head. He closed his eyes, but an image of Rachel flashed into his mind. Rachel with those wild auburn curls, those innocent brown eyes, those full, oh-so-kissable lips. He cursed under his breath, knowing sleep was going to be a long way off even though he was exhausted. His mind was spinning. Hell, he kept telling himself, it was only a kiss. So, he'd lost it for a moment. Big deal.

That was the problem. It *was* a big deal. Rachel was under investigation for murder, and the cop investigating her wasn't supposed to go around kissing her. At least, not this cop. He had rules, standards, ethics. Face it. He also had the hots for the very woman he was attempting to gather evidence against and have thrown behind bars.

He sat up in bed, bowed his head, dropped it into his hands. For a guy who prided himself on always having his feet planted firmly on the terra ferma, he was feeling like he'd lost his center of gravity.

Finally he got out of bed, shuffled into the kitchen, pulled a beer out of the fridge, and turned on the tube in the living room. WPIT was already off the air. He changed the channel and wound up watching some comedian doing a stand-up routine on an all-night comedy channel. The comic wasn't bad, but Delaney wasn't in the mood for laughing.

April 7

I couldn't believe it. Mellie thinking I actually have a crush on Delaney Parker. It was all I could do not to blurt out the way I really feel about him. Later that night I got Aunt Julie alone and told her all my suspicions about him, but she wasn't convinced. She says hit men always "stay out in the cold."

Okay, so he's not your run-of-the-mill hit man. At least Aunt Julie didn't discourage me from continuing my investigation. I was disappointed at first at not finding anything suspicious out at his house. But the more I think about it, the odder it seems to me that I didn't find anything. No pictures, no mementos, no letters. No personal stuff at all. It's like Delaney Parker dropped down out of nowhere. *Strange visitor from another planet* . . . Or a sinister creep from the underworld.

All night long, I've been racking my brain as to the next step in my investigation and it finally came to me. Monday, during recess at school, I'm going to place a call to Omaha, Nebraska. Supposedly, Parker worked at WROS out there. My mom says she's already checked out his references. But sometimes you need to check and double-check, as Aunt Julie once told me.

I just hope one day Aunt Rachel appreciates what I'm doing for her. And that I nail Parker before he nails—

Oh, God, I don't even want to have such an awful thought.

driver of the blue sedan, Delaney checked to see that

4

THAT MONDAY MORNING as Delaney watched Kate
Hart's house from a wooded piece of property belong-
ing to the home across the street, he couldn't shake the
feeling that he wasn't the only one who had his eye on
the place. A blue sedan had circled the block twice since
he'd been on his own stakeout. Then he remembered
seeing a sedan like that pass the house on Saturday
night when he and Rachel were on the porch. Interesting. He jotted down the number of the license plate.
     Shortly after eight, Delaney spotted Skye leave the
house, climb on her bike and take off down the street
for school. Kate and Rachel followed soon after, getting into Kate's car for the ten-minute drive to the station. As Kate's car pulled out of the drive, Delaney
checked up and down the street for a sign of the blue
sedan, but it was nowhere in sight. Nor did it circle the
street again during the hour wait before Julie emerged
from the house, hopped into her car, and took off. Had
the blue sedan followed Kate's car to the station? Was
the driver keeping a tail on Rachel? If so, whose orders
was he following? There were several possibilities—the
mob, the FBI, the cops. Delaney wouldn't put it past
Mendez, feeling under so much pressure, to send in reinforcements. Not that it pleased him to think Mendez
was worried he'd need backup. It pleased him even less

to think Mendez didn't trust him and had put the tail on him to make sure he was keeping his mind on business and not on Rachel's perfume. . . .

Putting aside his concerns about Mendez and the driver of the blue sedan, Delaney checked to see that no one was around before he dashed across the street and made his way around to the back of the house—a private little oasis bordered by shrubs and trees.

As he headed for the back door, he slipped on a pair of thin rubber gloves. If he came upon anything of interest, he didn't want to disturb possible fingerprints with his own.

It was no surprise to him that the kitchen door was unlocked. He knocked, just to be on the safe side. As expected, no one came to the door and he slipped right in.

He headed straight for the second floor. There was only one room he was interested in searching—Rachel's. Like the rest of the house, this room was a pastiche of New England country charm—a handmade quilt on the bed, Shaker-style furnishings, soft floral wallpaper, an oval rag rug on the wide pine flooring, ruffled white muslin café curtains on the two windows that looked out over the backyard.

The instant he stepped into her room, Delaney could pick up Rachel's scent—sweet and tangy at the same time. Intoxicating. It sent an involuntary flash of arousal through him. He quickly cursed himself for the way he was letting her get to him. He hurriedly told himself he'd get over it. And then his eyes spotted the cream-colored sweater she'd worn the other night on the porch. He remembered how the fabric had felt beneath his hands—soft, a little nubby. He remembered even more vividly Rachel's wonderful contours, her glorious lips.

He tried to think of Rachel Hart as a cold-blooded killer. He even shut his eyes for a minute and attempted to create an image of her, knife in hand, plunging it into Nelson Lang's back, a leering smile on her face.

No luck. *Okay, forget the leering smile. Change her from cold-blooded to hot-blooded. In the heat of fury and anguish, she impulsively picks up the knife, and before she can think straight . . .*

He couldn't picture it either way. That didn't mean anything, either, he reminded himself. A temporary malfunction in his "picture tube."

He shook his head, forcing himself to focus not on images, but on the job at hand.

Then, just minutes after struggling with images of Rachel as a killer had failed him, other images, equally potent but having nothing to do with murder, flashed completely unbidden into his mind. They started when he opened the top drawer of her bureau and saw all those soft, sensual, silk-and-lace undergarments of hers. A ripple of desire got the best of him; all of a sudden his eyes were closing of their own volition, and he was picturing Rachel standing in the room with him, dressed in one of those frilly floral silk bras and matching bikini panties. Funny, he didn't have any trouble at all picturing her as a tempting seductress. Or picturing himself slowly moving toward her, bare-chested, pulling her into his arms, drawing her bra straps down over her silky shoulders and exposing her breasts so they could be skin to skin—

He slammed the drawer shut, nearly slamming his finger in the process. What the hell was the matter with him? He caught a glimpse of himself in the mirror over the bureau. A bead of sweat had broken out across his brow. He scowled at his reflection, then yanked open another drawer so forcefully, it nearly fell out of the bureau.

Sweaters and jerseys in tidy piles. A little easier to handle. He got himself under control and worked in his typical, methodical fashion, lifting up each item, not sure what he was looking for or even hoping to find hidden away. Or was it hoping *not* to find?

He was lifting up the last sweater in the last pile when his hand and then his gaze fell on something that wasn't an item of apparel. It was a small leather-bound notebook. He had a distinctly uneasy feeling as he pulled the notebook out of the drawer, but before he opened the cover to see what it was he'd unearthed, he heard a noise behind him.

He swung around fast. Not fast enough to avoid the fist that landed square on his jaw.

Everything went black. No, there were little white spots first. Then it all went black.

The next thing Delaney knew, he was lying flat on his back on the floor, staring up into the face of a very wary twelve-year-old.

Delaney rubbed his jaw gingerly. "You've got some right hook there, kid."

"Don't be ridiculous," Skye snapped. "I wasn't the one that hit you. Not that I wouldn't have liked to," she added hotly. "What are you doing sneaking around in my aunt's room, snooping through her things?"

Delaney sat up. No use lying. He still had on those damn rubber gloves. Would the kid believe a skin allergy? *Hey, your Aunt Rachel sent me over here for some ointment....*

"It takes a snoop to know a snoop," was what he did say. "What were you doing snooping through my things last Monday?"

And she'd thought he'd never spot her search. She wavered for a moment, but then realized she was the one with the advantage here since she'd caught him redhanded. "I asked you first," she countered.

Delaney started to rise, but Skye snatched up a heavy marble box from the top of the bureau and waved it ominously over him.

Delaney stayed put. He was still a little woozy, and he didn't feature getting clobbered on the head after the solid hit he'd taken to the jaw. Besides, behind the kid's bravado, he could see that she was scared.

"Okay," he said, "let me ask you something else. Did you happen to see the character who did punch me in the jaw?"

Skye hesitated. Things were more confusing here then she'd bargained for. One bad guy was one thing. Two—well, that was double the trouble.

"It's important, Skye," Delaney said quietly. "Please tell me."

"Not exactly," she finally muttered.

"What does that mean?"

"I saw someone, but I didn't really pay any attention to him. He was getting into his car in front of the house."

Delaney raised an eyebrow. It hurt, so he lowered it again. "A blue sedan?"

Skye frowned. "Yes. How did you know?"

Delaney looked around the floor. "You didn't see a little notebook lying here when you walked in?"

"No," Skye said, then frowned again. "Hey, now it's your turn to answer my question."

"What question was that?" Delaney asked, buying time, wondering how he was ever going to explain to Mendez that he'd had his cover blown by a twelve-year-old wisp of a girl. He'd never live it down.

"I have quite a few," she said, raising the box ominously close to his head. "And don't think, because I'm a kid, you can pull the wool over my eyes."

"Okay, okay. I'll give you the whole scoop. But first I want to phone in the license-plate number of that blue sedan to the cops." He pulled off his gloves and again made an attempt to get up.

"Don't move," Skye warned, "or I'll clobber you, and I mean it."

"Look, all I want to do is use the telephone over there." He gestured toward the phone on the end table beside Rachel's bed.

"Uh-uh. How do I know you're going to phone the cops? How do I know that guy in the blue sedan isn't the cop? How do I know that you aren't . . . ?"

As she started spewing out questions, Delaney heard footsteps. Catching her off guard, he snatched hold of Skye's arm and yanked her down to her knees before she could strike out at him with the marble box. "Shh. Someone's coming," he whispered. From the sound of it, there was more than one of them. Had the character who punched him out come back with reinforcements "to tidy things up"?

An anxious voice called out, "Skye. Where are you?"

"Up here, Aunt Rachel. Hurry."

Delaney shut his eyes and sighed.

"Skye, are you okay?" Another anxious voice. Skye's mom. Great, Delaney thought. A regular three-ring circus. And he got to play the clown.

"I've got things under control," Skye called back, wriggling free of Delaney's grasp. When she was back on her feet she glared down at him. "I called Aunt Rachel and my mom. And the cops, too." She smiled smugly. "So now you won't have to bother to phone in that license-plate number to them," she added dryly.

Rachel and Kate practically tripped over each other, rushing into the room. They were followed by Pittsville's out-of-breath police chief, Lyle Woodrum, a heavyset man in his early forties, with thinning brown hair. The chief had his gun drawn, but Delaney could see he was awkward about handling it. Not very likely the local cops had many occasions to draw arms in this sleepy little town.

Kate made a beeline for Skye, but Rachel stood in the middle of the room, frozen, her eyes fixed on Delaney. She didn't say a word. She didn't have to. Her hostile expression said it all.

"I told you," Skye said. "I told you he was up to no good. He's got 'mobster' written all over his face. But would anybody listen to me? Noooo. I'm just a kid.

What do I know? Well, I happen to know he never worked for WROS, for one thing. For another—"

"How do you know that?" Kate interrupted. "I called the head of WROS myself and he confirmed—"

"I spoke to the secretary," Skye said, her turn to cut her mother off. "Oh sure, at first she said that a Delaney Parker used to work there. Obviously the mob paid them off to lie. But I caught her up in her little lie."

"How'd you do that?" the police chief asked. Kate was curious, too. As for Rachel and Delaney, their minds were on other things. They both remained mute.

"Simple, Chief," Skye said smugly. "I asked her if Delaney still had a weight problem. I mean, what with being only five feet four inches, carrying around three hundred pounds can put a big strain on your heart. She didn't know what to say then, so she just agreed with me. Five foot four. Three hundred pounds. Not exactly how I'd describe our Delaney Parker."

Skye beamed. So what if she'd gotten the idea from a cop show she'd seen on TV.

Kate glared at Delaney. "You bastard."

"Nice work, Skye," Woodrum drawled. "You're a clever girl."

Looking over at her niece, Rachel spoke for the first time. "You told me on the phone he was out cold."

"He was. I'd have done it myself, but someone else beat me to the punch," Skye said.

"Me, too," Rachel muttered sardonically.

Delaney didn't say anything. Nothing he could think of to say would have made matters any better.

"Why did you cut school and come home in the first place?" Kate demanded of her daughter. She tried to sound angry, but there was an unmistakable quiver in her voice. She was still a little shaken at the thought of what might have happened to her child if Skye had found this lying hoodlum conscious.

"After I spoke to that secretary at WROS, I knew something had to be done. I thought Aunt Julie would still be home, and I figured she'd know what our next move should be," Skye replied.

"This isn't a matter for your Aunt Julie," Kate said briskly. "It's a matter for the police."

The police chief nodded distractedly, then realized that meant him. He puffed out his chest and waved the gun at Delaney. "All right, get to your feet, young man. And keep your hands up in the air where I can see them."

Delaney's head started to pound as he rose. His stomach didn't feel all that great either, but that had nothing to do with the blow to the jaw he'd taken. He felt sick about having screwed up so royally. Sicker still, thinking about how Rachel had to be feeling about him at that moment. Then there was the matter of the guy in the blue sedan who'd knocked him out cold and waltzed off with that mysterious notebook he'd dug up in Rachel's sweater drawer. No one seemed interested or concerned about that guy or his prize—except him.

"Look," Delaney said, once he was standing, "you've got it all wrong. Rachel's in danger...."

"Not anymore she isn't," Skye said defiantly, arms crossed over her chest.

Delaney gave her a sharp look. "Use your head, kid. If that character in the blue sedan was a cop, why'd he knock me out and run off with the goods?"

Skye bit her lower lip. Good question.

"What goods?" the police chief demanded.

Delaney's eyes fell on Rachel. "You'll have to tell him. I didn't get the chance to look inside the notebook."

Rachel's throat was dry. Her gaze remained riveted on Delaney, but she didn't want to talk about that notebook now. She had only one thought in her head at the moment. "Did you kill Nelson?" she asked him straight-out.

Now why would she ask him if he'd killed Lang if she'd killed him? A clever ruse to shift the blame? Delaney didn't think so. Rachel simply wasn't the devious type. An answer that suited her—and him—better was that she was innocent.

"No," he told her with a smile, which came off a little crooked due to the throbbing pain in his jaw. "I didn't kill Nelson."

Rachel had no idea why he was smiling, but it didn't help his case any, if that was his aim.

"Who the hell are you?" she demanded.

"Yes," Kate said, joining in, giving him a look that was almost as hostile as Rachel's. "We'd all like to know that."

The police chief nodded solemnly.

"You can't believe a word he says," Skye said. "The thing to do is take him in, Chief, and fingerprint him. I bet, when you send his prints in, you'll turn up a rap sheet a mile long."

"I'm not the one with the rap sheet," Delaney said. "But there's someone cruising around Pittsville in a late-model, navy blue Ford, two-door sedan...."

"He's probably from a rival gang," Skye concluded, turning to the police chief. "Better put out an all-points bulletin—"

"Skye," Kate interrupted. "I think Chief Woodrum knows how to do his job. And you, young lady, should know better than to cut school. I'll drop you off back there right now." Kate looked over at her sister. "Coming, Rach?"

Rachel shook her head. "You go ahead, Kate. I'll meet you back at the station in a little while."

Kate hesitated. It was only seeing Skye's eagerness to stick around that made her take hold of her daughter's hand and drag her out.

When they left, Rachel's gaze once again fixed on Delaney. "You must think I'm the biggest jerk—"

"I don't," he said. "I don't think anything of the sort."

Rachel glowered at him. She was through believing a single word Delaney Parker—if that was even his real name—uttered. "You let me go on and on the other night. You let me flirt with you—"

"I wasn't absolutely sure you were flirting—"

"Liar."

"Rachel . . ."

Chief Woodrum cleared his throat. There was a lot more going on here than had first met his eye.

Neither Rachel nor Delaney paid any attention to the police chief.

"And all that talk about trust being a two-way street," Rachel went on. "Oh, you must have had yourself quite a laugh at my expense."

"I didn't laugh at all. I wouldn't laugh at you, Rachel. If I could have told you the truth, I would have."

"And what is the truth?" But she didn't let him answer. "You wouldn't know the truth if it fell on you," she added hotly.

"That's not true," he countered, his frustration rising.

"Oh, shut up," she snapped.

"Damn it, Rachel..." He started for her, but was quickly intercepted by Chief Woodrum's broad expanse.

"Hold it right there. And get your hands up," the police chief barked as he clumsily fished a pair of handcuffs out of his back pocket. "I mean, hands behind your back."

"Which is it going to be?" Delaney asked dryly.

"A liar and a comedian, huh?" Woodrum snickered.

"I don't find him the least bit funny," Rachel said. "If I was in charge, I'd lock him up and throw away the key."

"Okay, I lied to you," Delaney said as the chief cuffed his wrists. "But it's not what you think. I'm not one of the bad guys, Rachel. I'm one of the good guys."

"Now that's funny," Rachel said, emitting a harsh laugh.

"You want to come down to the station with us, Rachel," Woodrum asked, "and file a complaint? For starters, we've got him on breaking and entering—"

"I didn't break and enter. The door was unlocked," Delaney said.

"I see you've got a whole routine here," the chief muttered. "Too bad you didn't go into stand-up. Then you'd have only gotten booed instead of thrown in the clink."

Delaney looked over at Rachel. She was seething. He'd lost any gains he might have made in winning her trust. Trust. That was a laugh. *Yeah, trust me, baby. Pour your heart out to me. So I can throw the book at you.* Never had he felt so low.

He shifted his gaze from Rachel to Woodrum. "I'm a cop," he said with an air of resignation. This was the first time he'd blown his cover in ten years on the job. He had the uneasy feeling this was just the first of a lot of "firsts."

"Sure you are," Woodrum said, deadpan.

Rachel merely looked disgusted.

"It's the truth," Delaney insisted, looking over the chief's shoulder at Rachel. "I'm a New York City detective. I was sent here undercover to...to try to get to the bottom of the Lang murder." He didn't think it would help matters to be more specific.

"Next thing you'll be telling us you were up here in Miss Hart's bedroom doing a legal police search," Woodrum said, rocking on his heels. "That means you've got yourself a legal search warrant on you."

Delaney sighed wearily. "Well . . . no, but . . ."

"I didn't think so," Woodrum said with a humorless smile. "Let's go, son."

"And I honestly thought you had a meeting with some big-shot exec over at DMG&G," Rachel said forlornly, remembering where Delaney had said he was going to be that day. And she'd actually thought he was a brilliant salesman. Why not? He'd sold her a bill of goods, hadn't he? This was it, she told herself firmly. She would never again believe another man as long as she lived. They were all liars and cheats—the whole lot of them. Kate was right. You were better off without them.

Woodrum was leading Delaney out of the room. Delaney stopped and turned back to her. "I do have a meeting scheduled at DMG&G. I figured while I was playing the part of a sales rep, I might as well see if I couldn't bring the station in some sponsors."

"You're an even better liar than Nelson was," Rachel told him, her tone a mix of scorn and disgust. "If you want to take that as a compliment."

"Call there yourself, if you don't believe me. I had an eleven-fifteen meeting with Jim Bell," Delaney said. He turned to the police chief. "And you can call Homicide Chief Louis Mendez at—"

"Yeah, yeah, you can tell me all about it down at the station," Woodrum sneered, shoving him toward the door.

"Wait for me," Rachel said, hurrying after them. "I've got plenty of complaints to file against Delaney Parker."

CHIEF WOODRUM HUNG UP the phone, his rueful gaze shifting from Delaney to Rachel, both of whom were seated in high-backed wooden chairs on the other side of his cluttered desk. "His story checks out," he told her. "I spoke to Homicide Chief Mendez himself. Mr. Parker here is a New York City detective."

"See," Delaney said to her. "And you thought I was incapable of telling the truth."

Rachel sat there, mute. And steaming. Was she supposed to be elated that he was a cop instead of a mobster? Either way, he was up to no good as far as she was concerned. Whoever he was, he'd deceived her, tricked her, even wormed his way into her heart. A sucker again. What did she have—"gullible" written all over her face? When was she going to learn?

"Your chief doesn't sound any too happy with you, Parker," Woodrum said laconically.

Delaney scowled. "No. I didn't think he would be."

Woodrum looked across at Rachel. "You can still press charges. Being a cop—from New York City, at that—doesn't put him above the law. He did an illegal search."

Rachel pressed her lips together and shook her head. She didn't want to press charges against him. She simply never wanted to set eyes on him again. Rising without a word, she strode out of the office without so much as a backward glance.

Delaney sprang up to go after her. He not only very much wanted to see her again, he needed to. His cover blown or not, he knew Mendez wasn't likely to take him off the case.

"Parker," the chief called to him as he made a beeline for the door.

Delaney turned back to Woodrum, impatience etched on his face. "Yeah?"

The chief tipped back in his swivel chair, his arms folded over his ample belly. "You boys down in New York City think she did it? Killed that mobster?"

"She's . . . under suspicion."

"I've known her since she was knee-high," Woodrum drawled in his twangy New England accent. "You're on the wrong track."

"Believe me," Delaney confessed, "no one hopes so more than I do."

"Except maybe Rachel herself," Woodrum added with a knowing smile.

Delaney nodded. The chief was right, there. He started out the door.

"Aren't you forgetting something?" the chief called after him.

Delaney turned back again, puzzled. "What's that?"

"That blue sedan."

Delaney struck his temple with the palm of his hand. "Damn, I almost forgot all about that character." And about that little notebook he'd swiped. What he would have given for at least a couple of minutes to thumb through it before that creep punched his lights out. Now, he'd have to rely on Rachel to give him the low-down, and something told him not to hold his breath on that one.

First things first. He fished the paper with the license-plate number on it out of his slacks pocket, and handed it over to the local police chief.

"We'll get right on this," Woodrum said. "Shouldn't take too long. Why don't you wait?"

Delaney hesitated. He didn't really want to wait around. He wanted to go after Rachel and try to start mending bridges. *Hey Rachel, I'm sorry as hell I lied to you, but something tells me you wouldn't have been too thrilled if I'd told you the truth about what I was really doing here.* Oh yeah, he thought, that would really win her over, all right!

The police chief motioned to a seat, giving him a sage look. "Give her a little time to cool off."

Delaney gave the advice some thought, and finally shrugged. "Maybe you're right."

"It always works for me. And I've been happily married for thirty-three years."

Delaney crossed the room and sat back down while Woodrum had one of his men track down the name of the owner of the blue Ford.

"My guess is," Delaney said, "you're going to find that the owner reported his car stolen a few days back. And the creep who swiped it is probably long gone by now. My guess is he dumped the car off at the train station and hopped the express to New York." The same express *he* was supposed to have been on.

Delaney reached across the desk for the phone. "Mind?"

The chief shook his head.

Delaney flipped open a small address book and dialed a Manhattan number. A receptionist picked up after three rings.

"Yes, can I have Jim Bell's office, please?" Delaney asked.

Woodrum was observing Delaney closely as he waited to be connected.

Bell's secretary got on the line.

"This is Delaney Parker. From WPIT in Pittsville. I'm sorry to give you such short notice but I need to reschedule my appointment with Mr. Bell. A . . . family emergency."

The secretary was able to fit him in at the end of the week.

"Great," Delaney said enthusiastically. "Friday at one forty-five. I'll see him then. Thanks a lot."

Woodrum was shaking his head as Delaney hung up. "I don't get it. Your cover's blown. Why are you bothering to continue the masquerade?"

Delaney smiled. "I figure it's the least I can do. I actually think I can get their agency to fish up some sponsors interested in buying airtime on WPIT. If I can, well . . ."

Woodrum eyed him with a faint smile. "You always take your job so personally, Parker?"

"I never take my job so personally," Delaney confessed.

"I kind of guessed that."

The two men shared a look.

"I don't know what it is about her," Delaney muttered.

Woodrum grinned. "Oh, yes, you do."

Delaney felt the heat spread across his face. "Well..."

"I don't think Rachel's gonna let you off the hook too easy."

"I figure I'm gonna be on the hook until I can prove she didn't kill Lang, and nab the bastard who did."

"Sounds like a mighty tall order."

Delaney couldn't agree more. "And I don't have much time. Unlike the two of us, Mendez and the DA believe Rachel's guilty. If I don't come up with a better suspect soon, I'm pretty sure they're going to settle for Rachel. The DA's starting to think there's enough circumstantial evidence to book her as it is."

"Let me guess," Woodrum said. "He's holding off on your promise to Mendez that you'll come up with something more . . . substantial?"

"Well, they'd like some solid evidence."

"Like that little notebook you found up there in Rachel's room?"

Delaney gingerly rubbed his still-sore jaw. "Found and lost."

The chief's phone rang. He picked up on the first ring. After scribbling down a few notes, he hung up, giving Delaney another of his humorless smiles.

"The blue sedan belongs to a Victor Clafflin of Dennison. That's a little town about ninety miles south of here. Mr. Clafflin reported the car stolen last Thursday."

Delaney got little satisfaction out of having guessed right.

"I'll send a couple of my boys down to the train station and see if they spot the car," Woodrum said. "We'll check it for prints. Maybe we'll get lucky."

Delaney nodded, but the way this case was going so far, he didn't hold out much hope of any luck falling his way. Good luck, that was. Bad luck—he was swimming in it. Which brought his thoughts full circle to Rachel.

April 9

I can't believe it. I just overheard Kyle Woodrum, the police chief's son who's my phys-ed teacher, telling Beth Simmons, the girls' basketball coach, that Delaney Parker's not a mobster after all, but a cop. And not just any old cop, either. An undercover cop from New York City. No way Kyle could have gotten it wrong. He got the word from Lisa, his girlfriend, who's the police chief's secretary.

Delaney an undercover cop. Just like on TV. Boy, did I have him pegged wrong. Now it makes sense why he had no personal stuff back at his house. And do I feel dumb for having let the real mobster—the one in the blue sedan—get away. If only I'd paid more attention to him. I did catch a glimpse of him as he was getting into his car. He even looked straight at me for a minute, but I was too bent on getting into the house and relaying my big discovery about Delaney to Aunt Julie to notice important stuff like the color of his eyes or if he had any identifying scars. I do know he was tall and kind of bulky. Dark hair, definitely. Maybe with a little red in it. Or maybe it was just the way the sun was hitting it. Anyway, he's probably long gone by now. I blame myself. But how was I to know? Delaney should have leveled with me. I could have been a big help. In proving that Aunt Rachel didn't kill that nasty creep, Nelson Lang, that is. We could have teamed up. All that time I wasted.

Anyway, back to Delaney. I'm sure everyone's in a snit over his having lied to all of us—especially Rachel. To think he came here—infiltrated the television station, sat here having dinner at our dining room table, flirted with Aunt Rachel—and the whole time he was investigating her for murder. The flirting part was really low, because I think Aunt Rachel was getting a crush on him. I'm mad, too, but I've got to admit, I'm also impressed. The man's pretty good at his job. Except I'm definitely disappointed at how he let that character in the blue sedan get in that sucker punch and steal away with the goods.

Hmm. I wonder what those "goods" were all about? There must have been something that incriminated someone in that notebook, and that's why it was swiped. It could have been a diary. Nelson's diary. If Aunt Rachel swiped it from Nelson, then it seems to me she must know more than she's telling. Is there stuff in there that might not make her look so good? Is she trying to shield someone? Does she know who killed him, but won't say?

Or can't say? What if she's being blackmailed? What if she's afraid for her life? What if . . . ?

Oh, damn. The bell just rang. I've got to go to science class. We're dissecting a worm today. Murder and mayhem all around me and I'm stuck cutting up some slimy little creature. Life isn't fair.

5

"MEN," KATE MUTTERED derisively.

"Most men," Julie amended, eliminating her co-anchor and lover, Jordan Hammond, who she felt was above reproach. Or as above reproach as any man got.

"Delaney Parker goes to the head of the class," Rachel declared. Meaning, as they all knew, the class of *rats*.

Her two sisters nodded. No argument there.

Betty, who'd been waitressing for close to twenty years at the Full Moon Café on the green, catercorner to WPIT, topped off the three women's coffee mugs. "You can't live with 'em," she said, getting into the conversation, "but it's pretty darn dull without 'em."

"I'd settle for dull," Rachel said glumly.

"I *did* settle for dull," Kate said, "and no one hears me complaining."

Julie gave Kate a close scrutiny. "No one hears you cheering, either."

"You weren't cheering very much when the tabloids ran that photo of suave anchorman, Jordan Hammond, 'dirty dancing' with that hot little blond starlet, what's-her-name," Kate reminded her.

"They were not 'dirty dancing,'" Julie countered. "And Jordan didn't even know her. He was out in LA covering a story and he and his agent dropped into a club for a couple of drinks, and . . . what's-her-name . . . practically dragged him onto the dance floor."

"Uh-huh," Kate said, deadpan.

"You're just jealous," Julie said. "You think because you were married to a man who lied to you at every turn, that no man on earth can be trusted. Well, I trust Jordan. He's earned my trust."

Rachel placed her elbows on the table and cupped her chin in her palms. "I trusted Delaney. That is, I trusted my instincts about him."

"In your case," Julie said, "I think you'd be better off if you didn't trust your instincts when it comes to men, Rach. Not too long ago you were trusting your instincts about Nelson Lang. And look where that got you."

Kate nudged Julie in the ribs.

Julie winced, then apologized to her kid sister. "Sorry, Rach."

"No. You're right. If I hadn't gotten involved with Nelson, Delaney would never have entered my life, and I'd never have . . ." Rachel stopped abruptly, encountering the suspicious stares of her sisters.

She gave them an innocent look. "What?"

"You don't have any feelings for that sneaky, underhand, undercover cop, do you?" Kate's question was rife with accusation.

"Feelings?"

Julie squinted at Rachel. "It was one thing when you thought he was who he said he was, but now that you know he's a sneak, a bald-faced liar, not to mention that he's out to nail you for Nelson's murder, surely you can't still be infatuated—"

"Infatuated?" Rachel said indignantly. "Whoever said I was infatuated with Delaney Parker? I thought he was a nice guy. I thought he was attractive. I thought he was kind of sweet and earnest and there was something in his eyes.... A wistful yearning..."

"Oh, God." Julie sighed heavily. "It's even worse than I thought."

Kate gave Rachel a pitying look. "Oh, Rach, when are you going to learn?"

"I don't know what either of you are talking about," Rachel insisted, but she couldn't quite look either one of them in the eye. She popped up. "I've got to go or I'll be late for my appointment."

"OH, MR. PARKER. Delaney," Meg Cromwell called out as he raced down the hall at WPIT, heading for Rachel's office.

Delaney groaned as the television cook rushed to catch up with him. "My, you're in a hurry. I thought you were going to New York today. Did you miss your train?"

"Sort of," Delaney mumbled.

"Oh, how frustrating," Meg declared.

"Mrs. Cromwell, I'm in a bit of a hurry. I need to speak to Rachel."

"Rachel? She isn't here."

Delaney stopped short. "She isn't?"

"Why, no. She's got an appointment with..." Meg Cromwell leaned closer. "With her obstetrician," she finished in a whisper.

Why she was whispering was a mystery to Delaney since there wasn't another soul about. Not to mention that everyone in Pittsville, never mind the station, knew that Rachel was "with child."

"The obstetrician. Oh, right. She told me, but I forgot," Delaney lied. "What's his name again? It slipped my mind."

Meg Cromwell tsked. "George Moss. Over in Clark Mills. Personally, I don't see why she didn't go with Ron McCandless right here in Pittsville. He delivered both my boys, Lenny and Darrin, and I was very satisfied...."

"Yes, right," Delaney said distractedly, checking his watch. "How far is it to Clark Mills?"

Meg studied him thoughtfully. "You're going over there? To the obstetrician?" She forgot to lower her voice.

"Well, you see there are some papers—"

"Papers?"

"That I wanted Rachel to look at—"

"They must be very important papers."

"You don't know how important," Delaney said, heading for the exit. He was just out the door when Kate popped her head out of her office.

"That wasn't Parker, was it?" Kate demanded.

Meg Cromwell beamed at the station head. "That was him, all right. I do believe our new sales rep has fallen hook, line and sinker for your sister."

"The word's *stinker*," Kate muttered hotly, slamming her door shut.

DELANEY MADE THE fifteen-minute drive to Clark Mills in eight minutes. He pulled into a parking spot beside the offices of Drs. George Moss and Richard Taube, feeling a mixture of relief and anxiety at spotting Kate's car there. He hoped Rachel had borrowed her sister's car and driven herself over to the doctor's. He was going to have his hands full as it was, coping with Rachel, without having to deal with her big sister tossing in her two cents.

When Delaney burst into the cozy, pale yellow-painted waiting room, a half-dozen pairs of curious eyes looked up at him. One pair belonged to the slender blond receptionist seated behind a large maple desk in one corner of the room. The others belonged to the pregnant women seated in comfortable gray tweed armchairs awaiting their turns with the doctors.

Delaney smiled awkwardly at the group. His first "visit" to an obstetrician. At least Kate wasn't out there. Then again, she could be inside Dr. Moss's office with Rachel. The receptionist motioned him over to the desk.

"Can I help you?" she asked pleasantly.

Delaney placed his palms on the top of her desk and leaned a little closer to her. "I was looking for Rachel Hart."

She smiled brightly. "Oh, she's inside with Dr. Moss."

"Inside. Right. Well, I'll just wait out here—"

"You must be *Mr.* Hart. I'm sure it would be fine if you went inside. It's the first door on the left."

He looked in the direction she was pointing, but made no move. Nor did he make an effort to correct her.

"That's okay," he said. "I can..."

The receptionist was already buzzing Dr. Moss's office. "Mr. Hart is out here. He's feeling a little shy, but I'm sure he'd like to come in."

"Send him along," came the obstetrician's voice over the intercom.

Delaney flashed an uncomfortable smile. "I'll . . . uh . . . just go on in, then."

The receptionist grinned. "Let me guess. This is your first."

Delaney gave her a blank look. "Excuse me?"

"Your first baby."

Delaney ran his tongue across his lips. "Hmm. The first. Right."

RACHEL GAVE THE DOCTOR a puzzled look. "What's my father doing here?"

"Your father? Oh, I thought Ellen meant your husband."

Before Rachel could explain that she didn't have a husband, the door opened and Delaney walked in.

"Hi."

Rachel compressed her lips and glared at him. At least the exam was over and she was dressed. "What are you doing here?" she asked icily.

The obstetrician rose and extended his hand to Delaney. "Your wife got a little confused there. Thought it was her father come to see her."

Delaney shook hands with him. "No. No, I'm not . . . her father."

Rachel was about to say he wasn't her husband, either, but Dr. Moss was already telling Delaney that she was doing just fine and that he expected no complications to arise.

Delaney and Rachel shared a look. No complications? That was a laugh. Only neither of them cracked so much as a smile.

Dr. Moss folded his hands on the desk and focused his gaze on Delaney. "I imagine you'll want to be there at the birth."

Rachel's mouth dropped open. Delaney's clamped shut in surprise. When he managed to pry his lips apart, all he could manage was, "Well . . ."

"I've had a few fathers actually want to deliver the babies themselves. With my close supervision, naturally."

Naturally? Delaney stared at the obstetrician. There was nothing natural about this. He looked over at Rachel. Should he leave it up to her to explain, or should he? Before he could decide, the doctor was talking again.

Dr. Moss smiled. "I know. It all feels a little overwhelming right now. A lot of my fathers have the same look on their faces as you do when I bring up delivery, Mr. Hart."

Delaney doubted it was the same look.

"No reason to decide that now," the obstetrician said sympathetically. "We've still got five and a half months. Plenty of time for the two of you to talk everything over." He pulled open his drawer and withdrew a business-envelope-size pamphlet.

He slid the pamphlet across the desk. "Hope Hospital runs its own birthing classes and the two of you can sign up for one of them early on in your third trimester. You'll learn everything from breathing to meditation to massage techniques to diapering your baby and giving the tiny infant its first bath. Many of my mothers opt for natural childbirth, and as long as there are no complications, that's fine with me."

There they were, back to that word again. *Complications.* Everywhere Rachel turned there was nothing but complications. The biggest complication right now was Delaney Parker. Or, as Dr. Moss thought, Delaney Hart. Her husband. The father of her child. Hell, while they were at it, he might as well deliver the baby!

"LOOK, YOU CAN'T KEEP avoiding me, Rachel," Delaney said, his hand on her car door out in the physicians' parking lot.

"Avoid you?" She laughed sharply. "I can't seem to get rid of you for a minute. You're in my bedroom, you show up in my doctor's office. He thinks you're showing up in the delivery room. I'm afraid when I pull my shower curtain aside tonight I'll find you standing in my bathtub."

He smiled provocatively. "Now that's an enticing thought."

She spun around to him. "Don't you dare flirt with me, you . . . you cop."

"What do you have against cops?"

"Cops in general? Nothing. But you . . . You are another kind of cop altogether." She tried to open her car door, but Delaney's hand was still pressed against it.

"Let's go get a drink," Delaney coaxed. "There's a cute little place just up the road."

"Pregnant women don't drink."

"A soft drink. Pregnant women can drink sodas, can't they?"

"I'm not thirsty."

"How about something to eat, then?" His smile broadened. "Don't forget you're eating for two now."

"Don't you get it, Delaney? Do I have to spell it out for you?"

He caught hold of her by the shoulders. Something went a little haywire inside him. Rachel wasn't doing any better. Her chest heaved at his touch. Delaney could feel his pulse race.

"Don't you get it, Rachel?"

She stared at him, confusion, fear, anger, and an unmistakable hint of yearning reflected in her eyes. "No, I guess I don't," she said quietly. "You'd better spell it out for me."

"I was sent up here to try to get some hard evidence pinning you to the murder of Nelson Lang."

It took all of Rachel's willpower to keep her composure. "I didn't murder Nelson."

Delaney was still gripping her shoulders. He wasn't sure he could let go of her even if he wanted to. It didn't matter, since he didn't want to.

"I believe you," he said softly.

Rachel searched his face. "Why should I believe you?"

"Because I'm through lying to you. Because I want to win your trust, and this time I want to be able to deserve it. Because when that doc back there took me for your husband, it gave me this real funny feeling inside."

Rachel shut her eyes. Her head was spinning. "Don't do this to me, Delaney. I'm so damn . . . susceptible."

A breeze blew her wild auburn curls all over the place. The sun made her pale skin glow. "You're so damn . . . beautiful."

Her eyelids fluttered open. "Damn you, Delaney." She looked straight up at him. He looked straight down at her. Both of them were trying desperately to cling to their better instincts, but their baser instincts were rapidly gaining the upper hand.

"Rachel . . ." Her name was a mere whisper of desire. For an instant, before their lips met, somewhere in the middle, Delaney got a glimpse of her fear and longing—a perfect reflection of his own emotions.

His open mouth moved over hers. He could feel her lips trembling. His tongue touched hers. She let out a strangled moan. She could feel her pulse pounding in her head. She could feel the insistent beat clear down to her fingertips. Delaney knotted his fingers in her hair and she slid her hands around his neck. Their bodies pressed into each other, their tongues both actively involved now, eager to get reacquainted.

Pregnant women smiled at them as they came and went to and from their cars in the doctors' parking lot. Delaney and Rachel were oblivious. They were in another world. They kissed like it was a lost art and they were the artists rediscovering it.

The sudden blast of a car horn made them spring apart. Rachel had to throw her hand out against the car door to keep her balance. Delaney wasn't feeling altogether steady on his feet, either.

A very pregnant woman blushed as she got out of her car a few spaces down from theirs. "Sorry. Didn't mean to...disturb you. It's just this big old belly of mine keeps getting in the way."

Delaney and Rachel both cracked embarrassed smiles as the woman waddled past them. They were still smiling after she'd gone—like their smiles were glued on.

The smiles vanished in a flash when they looked at each other again.

Rachel's gaze quickly skidded off Delaney's face and she raised her eyes to the sky. "I can't believe this is happening to me."

Delaney's arms dangled at his sides. They didn't feel *right* there. They felt like they belonged around Rachel. "It wasn't something I counted on, either."

Rachel was slowly coming to her senses. Her expression turned icy. "No. You counted on sending me up the river."

"Rachel—"

"How could you think for one moment that I murdered Nelson? That I could murder anyone?" The ice turned to anguish.

"Does it help any that I started questioning it the minute I laid eyes on you?" he asked gently. He wanted to pull her into his arms again. He wanted to devour her lips again. He wanted to make love to her. A fine mess...

"And now you have no doubts at all?" she asked point-blank, her expression dogged.

God, what did she want from him? Absolute, unquestioning belief in her innocence. Yeah, he thought.

That's what she wanted, all right. The question was, Could he give her what she wanted?

Her gaze became so probing, he felt naked.

"Don't lie to me now, Delaney."

His heart was racing. His hands were clammy. It was his call. He knew he had to say it like he truly saw it, so he took his time.

Rachel waited. Never had an answer mattered as much to her—because she knew whatever he answered, she was going to believe him. It was crazy. She knew it. She'd barely allowed her vow to sink in about never believing another man as long as she lived—least of all, Delaney Parker—and already she was breaking it. She decided it was in her makeup. She needed to trust someone. She needed to believe in someone. No, not just someone. *Delaney.* She needed to trust him. She needed to believe in him. And she needed him to believe in her.

His gaze locked with hers. "I'm a cop, Rachel. I can't say...unconditionally...that you're innocent." He saw some of the glow go out of her eyes. But he had to give it to her straight. If there was ever a time in his life he needed to be honest with someone, everything in him told him this was the time. This was the someone. "I think a lot of people probably wanted Nelson dead—"

"And you think I'm one of them?" Rachel interrupted, her voice flat, lifeless.

"No. I don't think you *wanted* him dead."

"Well," she said, with no change in her voice, "I guess that's something."

He wished they weren't having this conversation. Since there was no avoiding it, he wished he could make it all better. He wanted to believe in her without a shadow of a doubt. Like she wanted. But all he could do was work toward it.

He needed something to go on. "What about that notebook, Rachel? The one I found in your bureau drawer? The one that creep who drove the blue sedan swiped from me after knocking me out cold?"

Rachel gave him a blank look. "I don't know," she replied.

"Rachel, I can't help you if you're going to hold out on me," he said with an edge of frustration.

"Look, I grabbed one of Nelson's small suitcases from the closet that night and threw some things in it. I didn't see that dumb notebook until I got to Kate's place and started unpacking. It was in one of those zippered compartments inside the bag. I just sort of glanced at it and tucked it away in my drawer."

"What was in it?"

She shrugged. "Lots of numbers. A few names. None of them struck a chord."

"Those names could be important, Rachel. You've got to try—"

"Not now, Delaney. My mind's—" She waved her hand around in the air. "Tell *me* something. Am I the star suspect in Nelson's murder, or... the *only* suspect?" Her voice wavered a little.

"What's important for now is that you're way at the bottom of my list, Rachel. Remember you told me you thought someone was outside when you left Lang's apartment?"

"I didn't actually see anyone. It was more a... feeling."

"Here's how it could have played out. You left the apartment like you said you did—with Lang snoring his heart out in bed. Someone was out there in the street—maybe that character in the blue sedan, maybe someone else—and when he or she saw you leave, they went upstairs and had a little meeting with your ex and it didn't work out the way they wanted—or it worked out exactly according to plan. And when they left the apartment, Lang was sprawled out on the kitchen floor, dead."

Rachel stared at him. "That's what you *think* happened."

He reached out tentatively for her. When his palm touched her bare arm, he was relieved that she didn't pull away. "Help me *prove* it, Rachel."

There was a long silence. Delaney didn't take his eyes off Rachel. Or his hand.

"And if you can't prove it?" she asked finally.

He could feel the sweat gathering across his brow. And it wasn't particularly warm out.

"We *will* prove it," he said emphatically. "You can bet the ranch on it."

"I don't have a ranch."

"Then what do you have to lose?"

Only her life.

Delaney's conviction was all Rachel had to cling to, however, and for all her conviction about standing on her own two feet, her legs were getting wobblier by the minute.

"Okay," she said a little wearily. "I'll do everything I can to help you find Nelson's murderer. I don't know how much help I'll be, but I'll give it my all."

He smiled at her. "No cop could ask for more." His smile deepened. "No man could ask for more."

Her lips parted. He was sorely tempted to kiss her again, but this wasn't the time or the place. Because he knew when he kissed her again, he wouldn't want to stop kissing her. He'd want to kiss every inch of her body. . . .

"So what do we do now, Delaney?"

"Well, we need to put our heads together."

A provocative sparkle glinted in her eyes. "Didn't we just do that?"

Delaney marveled at her. A woman whose life was on the line and yet could still crack a joke. This was no ordinary woman. This was one very special, incredibly unique woman.

It was at that moment that Delaney Parker fell in love with Rachel Hart. He didn't put that word to it. *Love* wasn't a word in his vocabulary—not defined the way he was experiencing it at that moment. It was just a feeling, but what a feeling. Pretty damn overwhelming for someone who'd seen it all and didn't "overwhelm" easily.

He faked a big grin, needing to downplay what was going on inside him. He wasn't even sure what it was, but he knew it was serious. "A regular comedienne, huh?"

Rachel got suddenly serious. "Only this is no laughing matter, is it, Delaney?"

His grin winked out. "No. No, it isn't," he agreed.

"I don't just mean the murder rap, Del." She was looking him straight in the eye. Open. Direct. Forthright. Honest.

Del. This was the first time she'd ever shortened his name. *Del.* The way she said it made it sound so intimate. So tantalizing.

"I know you don't," was all he said. It wasn't all he was thinking, though.

They stood there for a few moments in silence.

Rachel flashed an awkward smile. "I've got to get back to the station. Kate will start to worry."

"I'll follow you back."

"I don't know if that's such a good idea."

He arched a thick eyebrow. "You firing me?"

"Del . . ."

He opened the car door for her. She slid in behind the wheel and looked up at him. He was smiling.

"What's so funny?" she asked.

"Oh, I was just picturing you with a belly so big it touched the steering wheel."

"Pretty ludicrous-looking picture, I bet."

He shook his head slowly. "No. Not the least bit ludicrous."

He closed the car door and headed for his car.

Rachel just sat there, her hands white-knuckled on the steering wheel. She stared straight ahead, trying not to let utterly absurd fantasies crowd out the reality of her situation. All Delaney had said, after all, was that he didn't find the notion of her being very pregnant ludicrous. That was a long way from saying he'd like to make an honest woman of her.

An honest woman of her. What was she thinking? She was an honest woman. As her father always said— as honest as the day was long. Plenty of single women had babies these days. Sure, she believed it was better

for a child to have both a mother and a father, but that
didn't mean . . .

Was she really in the market for a father for her baby?
A husband? Had she settled on Delaney Parker—a man
she hardly knew? A man who'd lied to her? A cop sent
here to pin a murder rap on her? Okay, so now he'd
changed his tune. But if he couldn't prove she was innocent . . . ? He'd ducked that question. Rachel couldn't
duck it, though. If they couldn't come up with another
viable candidate, she was it. He'd have to bring her in.

Rachel concluded that she must be going nuts. One
kiss, a couple of compliments, and she was already
getting carried away. Delaney hadn't proposed marriage. He hadn't proposed anything except that they
work together to prove her innocence.

It kept coming back to that. She had to face facts. She
could still be arrested for Nelson's murder. She could
be found guilty. She could go to prison.

She glanced through the rearview mirror at Delaney, who was already in his car waiting for her to pull
out so he could follow her. Her lips still tingled from
their passionate kiss. If she was sent up the river, she
could ask him if he'd wait for her. . . .

JULIE WAS DOING SOME errands in town when she
bumped into her old high school pal, Leanne Sandler-
Nash, now six months pregnant with her second child.

"Well, I guess this is a two-for-one day," Leanne said.
"I saw your sister Rachel at Dr. Moss's office a little
while ago."

"Oh, really," Julie said distractedly. She had too much on her mind to get involved in a lengthy conversation with her old friend.

Leanne smiled conspiratorially. "So, what's the real story with Rachel?"

Julie gave the pregnant woman a blank look. Surely everyone in Pittsville knew the real story.

"I saw her husband, too."

Julie did a classic double take. "Her . . . what?"

"Quite a catch. So, why is everyone in town going around saying that Rachel's single? Why's she keeping her marriage a secret?"

"You must be confusing Rachel with someone else," Julie said.

"We talked before she went in to see Dr. Moss. Before her husband showed up and joined her in the doctor's office. And then when I was on my way out, I saw the two of them being very lovey-dovey in the parking lot. Like a pair of honeymooners."

Julie pressed her palm to her head. "I've got to go."

Flushed and out of breath, Julie raced into WPIT only to run smack into Leanne's big brother, Ben Sandler, in the hall. Julie and Ben went way back. Right to kindergarten at Pittsville's Marion Worth Elementary School. Well, actually, Julie had been in kindergarten with Leanne, but Leanne's irritating and irascible big brother, then in the second grade, used to always come around to their section of the playground during recess and tease all the girls. Some of them liked it. Some of them even swooned. Not Julie, though. She hated being teased by Marion Worth's pint-size "heart-throb," which, of course, made him do it even more.

The teasing didn't end in kindergarten. Ben just got better at it the older they got. He loved to provoke her, and Julie loathed being provoked.

"Whoa," Ben said, catching hold of Julie's shoulders. "Where's the fire?"

She gave her classically handsome, blond-haired nemesis an irritated look, nonetheless thinking to herself that probably half the women in Pittsville still swooned over the still-single, celebrated local television personality.

"I don't have time, Ben," she said brusquely, trying to wriggle free of his grasp.

The local news anchor was in no hurry to let go of Julie who was, to his mind, one of the sexiest anchorwomen on television today. And she looked even sexier in person. Especially in those hip-hugging black jeans and the formfitting cream-colored ribbed jersey accentuated with a wild Indian-print silk scarf. A mischievous smile tinged the corners of his mouth as he gave her an unabashed survey. "DC is growing on you, Jules." His smile deepened. "Looks like you've put on a couple of pounds."

Julie glared at him. "I haven't gained an ounce in three years."

He grinned. "Vanity, vanity. I thought you were the gal who said it's not how you look but how you look at things that matters," he teased.

"It has nothing to do with vanity. I was just stating a fact." As soon as the words were out of her mouth, she regretted them, knowing how defensive she sounded. Ben Sandler was one of the few people who could put her in that position. Usually she was the one on the attack, putting the other guy in the hot seat.

"Calling it like you see it?"

He just wouldn't let up. "Always," she said succinctly.

"What about getting together for dinner one night and reminiscing about old times?"

"What old times?" she countered.

He grinned seductively. "The ones we really had or the ones we only fantasized. You can take your pick."

"You'll never change, will you?" she said, rolling her eyes.

"Does that mean you will have dinner with me?"

"No. That means I have enough to deal with right now, without coping with your droll wit."

"Tell me, how's old Jordan's droll wit these days? Rumor has it you two aren't only burning up the airwaves together. Say, how about getting the old boy down here and I'll have the two of you on my show? It would be the biggest coup for 'Pittsville Patter' since I snagged Roy Higgs and his Famous Dancing Bears."

"He is not old," Julie said tightly. "He's only forty-two. He's in his prime. On camera. And," she added pointedly, "off."

"A good one, Jules."

"Now, if you don't mind..."

"I heard about the cop," Ben said, as she tried to sidestep him.

"I have to confess, Parker had me fooled," Ben went on. "When he came on board I thought he was totally straight-arrow."

"Well, he didn't have me fooled for one minute," Julie lied. "I knew there was something fishy about him." But even she hadn't guessed just how underhand he really was. Putting the make on Rachel—at her obstetrician's, no less—to win her trust. And from what Leanne had said, he'd won it in spades with very little effort.

"I haven't seen Rachel yet today. You don't think Parker... arrested her?" Ben asked with honest concern in his voice.

"No, he did something even more despicable," she muttered.

"What was that?"

"Oh, right. I'm going to blab to you and have it appear on the nightly news and maybe even as a feature on 'Pittsville Patter.'"

"That hurt, Jules. I happen to be very fond of Rachel. Always have been. I'm fond of the whole Hart family. Even you."

She felt a treacherous smile tugging at the corners of her mouth. For it all, there was something so irrepressible about Ben that in a rare weak moment she had, over the years, entertained some uncensored fantasies about him.

Reason fortunately won out. "Where's Kate? I've got to talk to Kate. I told her all along we couldn't just sit back and ignore this... crisis." She started for Kate's office.

"Kate's not in her office," Ben said. "She's in the control room with Mason Carpenter."

"Who's Mason Carpenter?"

"Her program director. He's trying out a shopping show. You know, like those shopping channels. Only this is strictly local wares being hawked. Kate's not all that crazy about the idea, but she's giving it a shot."

Julie started for the control room.

"Say, what about that dinner?" Ben called out.

"No time," Julie called back.

No sooner had Julie disappeared into the control room, than another Hart woman appeared on the scene. Ben greeted Rachel with a wave, relieved to see that she hadn't been arrested, after all. He started to tell her that Julie and Kate were in the control room, about to have a little powwow, when he saw Delaney Parker waltz in on Rachel's heels. Ben checked to see if the cop had her handcuffed. Her arms were swinging freely. She looked flustered, though. Like she didn't know which end was up. Not that Ben could blame her.

As Rachel and Delaney approached, Ben threw the cop an acid look. "Pretty dirty trick you played, Parker."

"Word travels fast," Delaney said dryly.

Ben clenched his fists.

"I wouldn't," Delaney warned. "One shot a day at being a punching bag is my limit."

"It's okay, Ben," Rachel said softly. "He's on my side."

Ben slowly unclenched his hands, continuing to eye Delaney suspiciously. "What do you mean, on your side?" he asked Rachel.

"He doesn't think I killed Nelson." Rachel didn't put the emphasis on the word *think*. She decided that Delaney would get more cooperation from everyone if they believed he had no doubt of her innocence.

"Hell," Ben said, "we all know that you didn't kill that slimeball."

Delaney smiled grimly. "Yeah, now all we've got to do is prove it."

"How?" Ben asked.

"Good question," Delaney countered.

"Ben, you didn't happen to notice a stranger hanging around the station since after I arrived here from New York?" Rachel asked. "He drives a blue Ford."

"No, I don't think so. A blue Ford?" Ben shook his head. "No, but I'll keep an eye out for him. What does he look like?"

Rachel glanced at Delaney, whose hand went absently to his still-sore jaw. "We don't know," she said. "We never got a close look at him."

"You think he's our man?" Ben asked.

Our man. Oh, great, Delaney thought. All he needed was to have everyone in Pittsville getting into the detective act. Things could get out of hand here real fast.

"I think I'd like to ask him a few questions," Delaney said obliquely.

"Listen," Ben said, "if there's anything I can do . . ."

The door of the control room opened, and Kate and Julie entered the hall. As soon as they spotted Delaney, they started for him like two fierce tigresses out to protect their young.

Rachel literally darted in front of Delaney, afraid her sisters might literally rip him to shreds. "Wait!" she shouted.

Julie and Kate started speaking—or shouting—at the same time, causing such a commotion that an agitated Mason Carpenter popped out of the control room.

"Please," the short, plump, bespectacled program director pleaded anxiously. "We've got a show airing. Charlie's pitching that truckload of cuckoo clocks Ellie Winchell ordered by mistake for her gift shop. The two phones are ringing off the hooks. I think we've got a real winner of a show here. We might have to install a couple more lines." He rubbed his palms together excitedly and ducked back into the control room.

Mason Carpenter's interruption broke the ranting rhythm of the two sisters, giving Rachel a chance to repeat for Julie and Kate what she'd told Ben Sandler about Delaney being on her side and wanting to prove she didn't kill Nelson.

They looked dubious.

"How do you know this isn't just a ploy to throw you off guard?" Julie demanded. "Cops are wily creatures, Rachel. They can set you up and you wouldn't even know what hit you."

One thing Julie said was true: Rachel didn't know what had hit her. But it didn't have to do with any fears of Delaney setting her up. It had to do with the way he'd kissed her; the way she kept wanting him to kiss her again.

Then she shook herself mentally. What was she doing, even thinking about kissing at a time like this?

"Men," Kate said bitingly. "First they knock you down and then they think they're heroes if they offer to help you onto your feet again."

"I'm the only one that got knocked down today," Delaney retorted wryly.

Julie gave him a deprecating look. "How long have you been in this game that you could get sucker punched like that?"

"You telling me no one ever caught you off guard?" Delaney countered.

Ben Sandler was tapping his finger against his lips. "I have an idea."

They all stopped to look at him. "What?" Kate asked.

"At the end of my six o'clock news broadcast, I could ask the illustrious citizens of Pittsville and the surrounding area if anyone out there has spotted that guy in the blue sedan. Then, if some folk come forward, I could interview them on 'Pittsville Patter' and . . ."

Delaney shook his head vehemently. "No. Now listen, folks. I'm sure you all want to help Rachel, but we're going to make more headway if we...keep a low profile for now."

"Oh, you mean like the one you've been keeping?" Kate quipped dryly.

April 9

Mom thinks I've been asleep for hours, but how can I sleep with all the excitement? I may never sleep again. A little while ago I snuck into Aunt Rachel's room. She wasn't sleeping, either. I wasn't surprised.

I decided to tell her what I could about that guy in the blue sedan. Not that I could give her much of a description, but at least it was something. You wouldn't believe the way she hugged me after I told her. She seemed to think it was a big deal. She said, "Wait until Del hears."

Del? She's calling him Del now. When my still-ex-friend Alice started calling Jeremy Froug "Jer" everyone in Edgar Rivers Middle School knew she had the crush of a lifetime on the conceited little jerk. And she was so gaga over him she didn't even know that Jer had a crush that whole time on Jen Shaeffer.

Del. Okay, I knew she was getting a little crush on him, but this could be more than a little crush. This could spell serious heartbreak for poor Aunt Rachel. Let's face it. How many men—a cop, no less—are going to want to get seriously involved with a potentially pregnant murder suspect? No, that didn't come out right. I don't mean "potentially pregnant." I mean a "potential murder suspect who's definitely pregnant."

I hope it's a girl. I hope she doesn't end up with a mother who's stuck in "the big house" for years making license plates. If only I could dig up some more clues. Whatever Aunt Rachel thinks, I'm not about to sit around and put all my trust in *Del* to clear her good name. You can bet on that.

PS. It still makes me boiling mad to think that when I teased Alice about her crush on Jer, she accused me of being jealous because I felt the same way about him. I *never* had a crush on Jer. And whatever Mellie Oberchon thinks, I *do not* have a crush on Del!

6

DELANEY'S STOMACH WAS churning as he gripped the phone. "Yeah, I know they're all breathing down your neck, Chief, but I'm telling you this isn't an open-and-shut case. Hold off for a couple of weeks on issuing a warrant for her arrest. You don't have any more proof now that she did it than you did a week ago."

"The DA thinks we can get an indictment. There's enough circumstantial evidence—"

"Not enough to make his case stick. Give me a couple of weeks, Chief. I'm telling you, there's more here than meets the eye."

"We don't have a couple of weeks, Delaney. And I gotta tell you, I'm a little disappointed in you. No, I'm plenty disappointed."

"Hey, like no one's ever snuck up behind you and laid you out? Like you've never been caught off guard, Mendez?" If the line worked on Rachel's sister, maybe it would work on his boss, too. It was worth a try, anyway.

"I'm not talking about that, pal. What I'm talking about is that you're losing your professional detachment out there."

"Because I don't want to pin a murder-one rap on a woman I think could very well be innocent?" Delaney charged, an unswallowable lump gathering in his throat.

"Because of what I'm hearing in your voice. Because I think that, just maybe, you've got the hots for our star suspect."

"You don't know what you're talking about." Delaney only wished. The problem was, Mendez knew exactly what he was talking about.

"The DA says he'll settle for murder two," his chief said.

"Oh, great."

"I'll hold off on the warrant for a couple of days."

"A week," Delaney bargained, his chief reluctantly agreeing.

"Don't do anything stupid," Mendez cautioned. "Even cops a lot smarter than you have been fooled by a pretty face. And you're plenty smart."

"Thanks for the compliment," Delaney said dryly, clicking off before Mendez beat him to the punch. Then he rolled over, switched off the light, and beat his pillow into shape. Just as he was starting to drift off, he heard a faint rapping sound.

He sat bolt upright, instantly wide-awake although it took him a few seconds to realize the sound was coming from someone knocking lightly at his front door.

He glanced at his alarm clock. It was almost one in the morning. Who the hell . . . ?

He grabbed a pair of jeans and put them on. On his way to the door, he also grabbed his gun. He wasn't about to leave himself open for another little surprise.

Surprise, however, was written all over his face when he cracked open his door and saw Rachel standing there. She was wearing a pair of red running pants and a gray sweatshirt with the words Run For Your Health emblazoned in red across her chest. He mentally x-ed out the word *health* and changed it to *life*. Run For Your Life....

The expression on her face—nervousness, worry, agitation—fit his amended inscription.

"What is it? What's wrong?" he asked, a cold blast of mountain air reminding him he was standing there bare-chested. Just like in his fantasy up in Rachel's room earlier that day. Even though he was thrown at finding her at his door at that hour, he fleetingly wondered if she was wearing any of that frilly underwear he'd spotted in her drawer.

"Did I wake you?" she asked anxiously. Her eyes drifted down his bare chest and then she caught sight of the gun in his hand. Her mouth dropped open.

Delaney quickly stowed the weapon in his front right pocket. "No. No, I was wide-awake."

"Can I come in?" she asked hesitantly.

"Yeah, sure," Delaney said, stepping aside from the door, his arms crossing his chest as his hands attempted to rub off some of the goose bumps that had popped up on his skin. Half of them were a result of the chilly night air; the other half, a result of Rachel's unexpected arrival.

She stepped into the tiny vestibule. On the right was the living room, beyond which was Delaney's bedroom. On the left was a small dining room that led on to the kitchen.

She turned right into the living room, a spare space consisting of a Colonial print couch, a brown corduroy wing chair and a couple of tables, on one of which sat a thirteen-inch color television. Delaney followed her into the room.

"I probably should have waited until morning," she said with a note of apology in her voice.

He started for the open door of his bedroom. "I'll just go put . . . a shirt on."

"It probably isn't much, but—" she followed him absently as she spoke "—it turns out my niece, Skye, actually did get a brief glimpse—" She stopped short as she found herself standing in the middle of Delaney's bedroom. Her gaze fell on his bed, the rumpled sheets, the covers flung back, the indentation in his pillow. "I *did* wake you."

Delaney was reaching for a blue denim shirt from the back of the chair beside his bed. "No. I was just...lying there."

Rachel smiled faintly. "I couldn't sleep, either."

Delaney forgot about his shirt. He forgot about the description Rachel had come there to give him of the guy in the blue sedan. He forgot about everything except that it was the middle of the night and this incredibly beautiful, desirable woman was standing there in his bedroom. He sure as hell hoped this wasn't a dream. Or if it was, that he didn't wake up for a while.

Rachel was having her own problems remembering what she was doing in Delaney's bedroom at such an ungodly hour. She was acutely aware of the thump, thump, thump of her heart, and of the way the moonlight filtered through the off-white café curtains and played over Delaney's broad bare chest, making his skin gleam.

She could have turned away and walked back into the living room, primly sat herself down on the sofa and waited for him to put his shirt on and join her. Probably wiser still, she could have left his house altogether, telling him it was dumb to have come over there in the middle of the night when what little she had to say could certainly wait until she saw him—anyplace but in his bedroom—the next day.

If only he would stop looking at her the way he was looking at her. Not like a man on the make. That was a familiar-enough look to her. That was a look she could handle with her eyes closed.

No. Delaney wasn't wearing one of those typical leering expressions. He was looking at her like a man drowning in anguish and longing. He was looking at her like a man who wanted to scoop her up in his arms and bolt out the window—both at the same time. He had fear and desire scribbled all over his face so it was hard to decipher one from the other. Rachel was no handwriting expert but she could read what was going on with Del, because looking at him was like looking at a reflection of herself. They were both fighting the same battle.

And she knew, just like she knew he knew, that they were both going to lose it. Sometimes, though, you had to lose a battle to win the war.

Slowly, he walked over to her, still holding the denim shirt in his clenched fist. Rachel looked up at him.

"Some people might think I'm out to compromise you," she said quietly.

"It's only what *I* think that counts here," he murmured.

"What *do* you think?"

"I think," he said, pausing to kiss her forehead, then her cheek, then the lobe of her ear, "that I've never wanted a woman as much as I want you."

She smiled without artifice. "I guess this is the real reason I showed up here tonight."

He kissed the side of her neck, sweeping aside a tangle of curls. "You think?"

Her arms slipped around his neck. "I know."

He let his shirt drop to the floor, lifted up her sweatshirt and drew it over her head. She wasn't wearing one of her lacy bras. He wasn't disappointed, though. What he saw was even more than he'd anticipated. She wasn't wearing anything under the sweatshirt. His earlier fantasies hadn't done her justice. She was exquisite. The sight of her took his breath away. Her breasts were fuller than he'd imagined, wonderfully firm. He lowered his head. The taste of those nipples was pure elixir. Sometimes reality was even better than fantasy. . . .

Rachel moaned softly, arching into him, her fingers trailing slowly, tantalizingly down his bare back. "Oh, that feels so good, Del," she whispered unabashedly. She smoothed his hair off his forehead, pressed her moist lips against his temple.

It wasn't until he began to draw her running pants down over her hips, making visible the gentle swell of her abdomen in the pale moonlight, that Rachel came back down to earth.

Delaney sensed her shift in mood instantly and dropped his hands to his sides. "What is it? What's wrong? Isn't it okay to . . . ? I mean . . . did your doctor . . . ?"

"It's okay," she said quietly, then hesitated. "If it's okay with you."

Del didn't get it. "Okay? Rachel, it's more than okay. I told you, I want you. . . ."

"I thought, maybe in the heat of the moment, you might have forgotten about my being pregnant."

He placed his palm gently over her stomach. The skin felt like velvet. He couldn't believe the softness of her. "I didn't forget. It doesn't matter, Rachel." He frowned. "No, that's not right. It does matter. I don't know what you're going to think of me for saying this, but I want to be straight with you from now on. No lies, no evasions, no pretense."

Rachel's breathing turned shallow. "Tell me, Del." She expected him to confess that he was troubled by her being pregnant with another man's child; that it did affect his feelings for her, even his desire. She told herself she'd take whatever he told her stoically, then throw her sweatshirt back on pronto and get out of there before she made an even bigger fool of herself.

"I find your being pregnant . . . a turn-on," he said with a sheepish smile.

"What?" Rachel couldn't believe she'd heard him right. Surely he'd said, "A turnoff."

Del stroked her gently rounded stomach lightly with the tips of his fingers. "It . . . arouses me. I think of that baby growing inside you, Rachel, and it's such a wondrous thing. It's life. I used to hear people say that women, when they were pregnant, exuded a special glow. That no matter how plain or even how beautiful they were before, during their pregnancy their beauty intensified." He combed his fingers through her wild curls, pulling them away from her face. Then he pressed his lips against her hair. "You are the most beautiful woman I've ever laid eyes on, Rachel."

Tears spilled down her cheeks. "Oh, Del. You've gone and plucked me right out of my nightmare and into a dream. I know we're both going to have to wake up, but I need that dream for a little while. I need it desperately."

Her lips quivered as they parted. Delaney's mouth moved over hers for a kiss he'd been aching to repeat all day. This one was even better. As fiery as the kiss they'd shared in the parking lot had been, this one was a real scorcher. Especially with her bare breasts pressed against his naked chest.

Still kissing her, he tugged her jogging pants down lower, with Rachel helping, until they were down around her ankles. She tried to kick them off, but couldn't because of the elastic around the cuffs. Meanwhile Delaney was trying his best to squirm out of his jeans, but they, too, had gathered around his ankles. They both started to lose their balance.

"Some dream, huh," Delaney teased playfully as they clutched each other to keep from toppling to the floor.

"This isn't the way it is in the movies," Rachel said, laughing as together they hobbled over to the bed a few feet away. Del eased Rachel onto the mattress, then he dropped to the floor to wrestle first with her running pants, then with his tight-cuffed jeans. The whole time his fingers were trembling, making his efforts all the more difficult. He finally managed to rid them both of their confining garments.

When he got to his feet, Rachel made a grab for him and he fell onto the bed, half on her, half beside her. She laughed again. She had an incredible laugh—earthy and sensual yet girlish and sweet at the same time. For a moment, Delaney felt close to tears. It was almost too much for him.

Sharp arousal, intensified by Rachel's long, sinuous strokes down his back and over his buttocks, nipped those emotions in the bud. His whole body shuddered with pent-up longing. He lifted himself off her enough to take in the whole length of her body. Perfection, pure and simple. He drank in her beauty like a desert wanderer who'd found his oasis. His lips cruised her face, her sweet persimmon-tinted lips, the long, graceful column of her neck.

Rachel wrapped herself around Delaney, feeling equally aroused and excited by his lanky, lean but muscular body. It was more than pure physical attraction, although she wasn't denying that was there in spades. The "more" had to do with the measure of the man himself. Even though his undercover work had required him to lie and deceive people, Rachel believed that Delaney was basically honest, decent, and caring. She also sensed a yearning in him for something—a completeness that had eluded him, a deeper sense of purpose, a drive to find more meaning in his life.

"Rachel," he whispered, the sound like music to her ears. She could feel all her muscles trembling, a throbbing sensation radiating throughout her body. Whatever nightmares awaited her tomorrow and the days after that, no one could ever take this dream night away from her.

"Oh, Del," she murmured, awash with a consuming hunger for him. She wanted him desperately, but she didn't want it to end too fast. With a tantalizing wantonness, she let her hands and lips explore the wondrous topography of his firm, muscular body.

He groaned as she caressed him. It had been a while since he'd been with a woman. It had been longer still since he'd been with a woman that even came within a mile of making him feel the way Rachel made him feel— wild with desire, yet fiercely protective. He had never before seen himself as particularly tender, but Rachel made that quality seem to spill right out of him.

His hands cupped her full breasts. She placed her hands over his. "They've grown some with the pregnancy," she said shyly.

He pictured a baby suckling from her nipples and it nearly brought him to tears. The feeling was palpable. He stroked her voluptuous breasts, knowing that he'd revel in them, no matter what their size.

She sought his mouth now, starved for the taste of him. Their kiss was moist, heated, each of them taking delight in knowing it was merely a preamble to the main event.

They were still kissing as he entered her, Delaney on top of her, Rachel's arms and legs wrapping around him. His mouth encompassed her as his body did. She couldn't breathe, but it didn't matter. Nothing mattered but these wild, intoxicating sensations that were consuming her. Her body felt heavy and languid. Delaney's body felt wondrously tough and vibrant.

First there was a gradual letting go, but they were both so inflamed they very quickly lost all control. Neither of them could catch their breath as their rhythm intensified. Then, when they found their voices, all they could emit were cries of pleasure. Soon they were positively shrieking, and the crazy thing was that neither of them had ever before been what could be called "vocally expressive" when it came to sex.

This went way beyond sex. This was what lovemaking was all about. Delaney had never truly experienced it before. Rachel had only thought she had. Now she knew the real thing.

Afterward, she curled against him and he held her very lightly, his palm once again resting on the gentle swell of her stomach. Rachel started to drift off. Delaney was stroking her hair, marveling at how much he already wanted her again, when suddenly she sprang up to a sitting position.

"Thomas!" she exclaimed.

Delaney was thunderstruck. Here he thought he'd just had the most meaningful experience of its kind in his whole life, and the woman he'd experienced it with couldn't even get his name straight?

"Del," he reminded her dryly. "Or Delaney will do." Hell, he'd settle for Parker.

"What?" Rachel said distractedly, turning around to face him.

Great. He was going to have to repeat it. "I said . . ."

"John," she declared, glowing with excitement.

First Thomas. Now John. He was past being affronted. He was starting to worry that Rachel wasn't all there.

Rachel hugged him. "Oh, it probably doesn't mean much, but . . ."

Delaney pulled her away from him. "Oh, it means something, all right," he said archly.

Rachel's eyes widened. "You mean you know him? You've heard of him?"

Delaney's brow furrowed. "Know who?"

"John Thomas."

"Who's John Thomas?"

"Wait a minute," Rachel said. "Didn't you just say . . . ?" She squinted at him. "This is starting to sound like the Abbott and Costello 'Who's on first' bit. Let's start over again."

"Let's," Del agreed enthusiastically.

"Remember, earlier . . ."

"It's not my memory that needs questioning, here."

"Come on, Del. This is no time for jokes. I'm being deadly serious." She shut her eyes for a moment and shuddered. *Deadly,* was right.

He propped two pillows behind his head and folded his arms over his bare chest. At the same time he tried to keep his eyes off Rachel's bare chest. He was damned if he was going to start having any further erotic fantasies about a woman who couldn't even get his name straight. Or anything else, it seemed.

"Please, Del."

He gave her a point for getting his name right this time. Plus, those erotic fantasies were getting the bet-

ter of him despite his efforts. "Okay, okay. What am I
supposed to remember about earlier?"

"I don't mean earlier tonight. I mean way earlier today. Outside my obstetrician's office. When you asked
me about that notebook of Nelson's that I accidentally
ended up with . . . temporarily."

Delaney nodded slowly, the light starting to dawn.
"The names in the book. John Thomas . . . ?"

Rachel grinned. "John Thomas was one of the names.
It appeared several times. Now that I think about it, I
remember Nelson speaking on the phone several times
to someone he called John."

"What kind of talk?"

Rachel shrugged. "I'm not sure. Nelson always
wanted privacy when he was on the phone, so if I accidentally walked into a room and he was speaking to
someone, I didn't stick around for very long." She
compressed her lips. "One time when he was on the
phone with this guy he called John, it did sound like
Nelson was angry. It was a very controlled anger,
though. In all the months I was with Nelson, I never
once saw him really lose his temper. I did notice, that
particular time, though, that his voice was a little
tighter and hoarser than usual."

"And you're sure he was talking to John?" Delaney
prodded.

"Yes." Rachel's eyes lit up. "It's coming back to me.
See, on that particular day I wasn't expecting to find
Nelson home. I thought he was on one of his . . . bird-
watching jaunts. Anyway, when I walked into the
apartment and saw him there, I got real excited and I
didn't realize at first that he was on the phone. When I

saw that I'd interrupted him, I apologized and started to go off to another room, only I dropped my purse and some stuff fell out and it took me a few seconds to pick everything up. First, I heard him say, 'Hold on a sec, John.' Then John must have said something that irritated Nelson, because that's when his voice got tight and hoarse and he said something cutting. . . ."

She closed her eyes and tried to recapture the conversation in her mind. It was no good. She couldn't remember what it was that Nelson had said. Except for one thing. "The second time, he didn't call him John. I'm almost positive he called him Thomas. It makes sense that Nelson would use the guy's last name if he was annoyed, doesn't it?"

Delaney smiled at her. "It makes a lot of sense."

"So, now what?"

"Tell me. Did you ever meet this John Thomas? Did he ever come to Lang's apartment? Or did you meet socially somewhere? Or . . . ?"

"No. Nelson and I didn't go out much. And when we did, it was usually just the two of us. We'd go out to dinner. Or a movie."

"And Lang never left you for a few minutes, say at a restaurant, to have a little chat with someone at another table? He might have told you he was just going to say hi to a fellow bird-watcher."

Rachel shrugged. "I can't remember any specific time. Even if it did happen, how would I know it was Thomas he was speaking to?"

She saw him frown and wished she could have given him something more concrete.

"I guess it isn't much, is it?" she said apologetically.

Delaney's frown disappeared and he hugged her. "Baby, you did great." One arm still around her, he snatched up the phone.

To say that Louis Mendez was less than thrilled to be getting another call from Delaney Parker in the middle of the night would have been an understatement.

Delaney quickly apologized. In the excitement of getting his hands on a downright clue in this murder case, the time had actually slipped his mind.

Mendez barked right through Delaney's apology, his voice carrying loud enough for Rachel to hear.

"He sounds pretty angry," she observed.

"Naw, he always sounds that way," Delaney quipped, holding the receiver a few inches from his ear and slapping his palm over the mouthpiece.

As soon as Mendez stopped to catch a breath, Delaney spoke his piece. "You did say I could call you day or *night* if I had something. I have something."

"It better be good."

"John Thomas."

There was silence on the other end of the line. Delaney smiled reassuringly at Rachel, then he repeated the name.

"That's it?" Mendez muttered. "Are you going psycho on me up there, Delaney? Or is it that dame again? I told you she'd have your head spinning. Didn't I warn you?"

Rachel grinned, gliding her fingers lasciviously up Delaney's thigh. "So I've got your head spinning?" she murmured seductively into his ear. Delaney caught hold of her hand before she'd moved it too far for him to be able to think straight.

"Say, are you alone?" Mendez asked suspiciously.

"Of course I'm alone," Delaney quickly retorted, avoiding Rachel's wry smile. "It's the middle of the night."

"I know what time it is," Mendez snapped.

"Come on, Chief. John Thomas. I know. The name didn't grab me right away, either. Think back to that east Brooklyn mob war a couple of years back. One figure who kept way in the background was this character, Jonathan Thomas II. He was a big shot at some record company. Delta. That was it. Delta Records."

"Yeah, right. I remember. He was a real shrewd dude. Made sure his hands were clean so nothing could get pinned on him."

"Did you know Thomas and Lang were buddies?"

"Buddies?"

"Well, that they did some business together anyway," Delaney said, knowing he was inferring a lot more than he had any business inferring from the little tidbit Rachel had given him.

"Is that right? And how do you know that?" Mendez asked.

"Rachel saw—"

"She saw him?" Mendez interrupted. "She saw Thomas and Lang together? What does she know about the business they were involved in?"

"Slow down. First thing I want to do is have a little chat with Thomas. How about arranging for him to come down to the station house for some questioning, say around two tomorrow?" Delaney yawned. "I'd make it earlier, but I'm really beat." He smiled at the woman who was the cause of his exhaustion, sitting there in all her naked glory, making him think that if he was beat now, he was also incredibly aroused again, which meant he'd really be zonked in give or take another hour.

"You're beat?" Mendez grumbled. "I'm the working stiff that's got to be down at the station by nine, Delaney. You can sleep your whole morning away, now that you've so conveniently blown your cover."

"I haven't blown it entirely. That is, I've blown it, but I'm still kind of keeping a hand in." At that particular moment his hand was involved in another kind of activity altogether; it was following the tantalizing curve of Rachel's hip.

"What does that mean?" Mendez asked.

"Being a TV sales rep has a certain appeal," Delaney said with a smile. "I've got another appointment on Friday with that big-shot advertiser you connected me up with in Manhattan."

"You mean you're really gonna try to sell television time in the middle of working on this case that the DA and the mayor are crawling all over me about?"

"Don't worry, Chief. I guarantee you, this case is going to get my wholehearted involvement," Delaney emphasized as Rachel snuggled against him.

"All right," Mendez spat out, resignation in every syllable. "I'll check and make sure this Thomas character's in town and that we can get him here by two, tomorrow. I'll call you first thing in the morning to let you know."

Delaney grinned. If his chief wasn't going to get much shut-eye he'd make sure he wouldn't, either. "You might want to have Kelso run a check on Thomas, as well."

"I already thought of that," Mendez replied.

"Oh, and I thought I'd bring Rachel along."

"You thought you'd what?"

"Speak to you tomorrow morning, Chief. Hey, get some sleep, okay?" Delaney said and then hung up.

"You want me to come to New York to question Thomas with you?" Rachel asked.

"No. I want you to sit behind a one-way mirror while I question Thomas and see if you recognize him. If you're up to it."

"Why wouldn't I be up to it?"

Delaney smiled lecherously. "Because I intend to keep you up awhile longer and you might be too tired," he said pulling her back down with him on the bed.

April 10

Got up early and decided to peek in on Aunt Rachel on my way to the bathroom. *She wasn't there.* Okay, I told myself, don't panic. I checked her bedroom and I didn't see any sign of a struggle. Then I snuck downstairs and saw that Aunt Rachel's bike was missing. An early-morning bike ride? Hmm. I wonder if she decided to bike down Millbrook Road to the old Seymour place, now being rented by Delaney Parker. Think I'll throw some clothes on fast and bike on down there myself before school starts.

Uh-oh. I just heard Mom stirring. Better dash off a note to her about how I went to school early to go over some homework with Alice. Mom doesn't know Alice and I aren't speaking. I guess that sort of makes it a *double* lie. Okay, I'll say it's Nadine. Then again, Nadine and I aren't exactly on the best of terms, either. She keeps bugging me to make up with Alice, but I think if there's any making up to be done, it should be done by Alice, not me. I won't say who I'm going over the homework with. One lie is better than two. I do hate to lie. I promise, once Aunt Rachel's in the clear, to work doubly hard at telling the truth.

7

AT SEVEN THE NEXT morning, Rachel and Delaney were rudely awakened by a commotion outside the small cottage. Groggily, Delaney dragged himself out of bed and shuffled over to the window.

"Oh my God," he muttered in disbelief.

"What is it?" Rachel asked sleepily as she rolled over.

"I don't believe this. I'm being . . . picketed."

Rachel sat up in bed, rubbing her eyes. "What?"

"Your dad's out there. And there's his girlfriend. Along with about twenty or more Pittsville locals, it looks like."

Rachel blinked in confusion, then wrapped the blanket around her naked body and joined her "bedfellow" at the window. One look at the two dozen or more people gathered outside on his front lawn—all of whom she knew, at least one of whom she was related to—each carrying homemade placards proclaiming her innocence of all wrongdoing, and she spun away from the window in horror, flattening herself against the wall. "Oh my God."

Delaney grinned ruefully. "Exactly."

"This can't be happening," she said, dazed. "I must be dreaming." Her eyes shot to the alarm clock on the table. Ten minutes after seven. How had it gotten to be that late? At around two that morning she was just going to shut her eyes for a few minutes, to savor those wondrous moments of passionate lovemaking with Del. She'd never planned to fall asleep and spend the whole night with him. She'd meant to be back at Kate's place long before everyone woke up. If only she hadn't dozed off. She hadn't slept so soundly in weeks. Months. Ages.

"I guess it's got to feel good to know you've got so many supporters literally willing to go on the line for you," Delaney commented with a smile.

Rachel was beside herself. "Feel good? Feel good? Are you kidding? What are they going to think if they know I'm here? This is a small town, Del. My father's out there, for heaven's sake."

Delaney gave her a baffled look. "I don't get it. You lived with a mobster for six months and you weren't tarred and feathered."

"That was in New York. And Nelson and I had . . . an understanding." Rachel scowled. "Well, I thought we had an understanding, but that's because I didn't understand anything about the things Nelson thought I understood and which I should have understood. Only I didn't . . . until it was too late. I don't mean too late in the too-late, Nelson-is-dead sense. I mean too late in the sense that if I'd had any sense in the first place."

Delaney stood there watching her in amusement. "Are you always like this the morning after?"

Rachel ignored the question. "Besides," she went on, "everyone back here thought Nelson was this sweet, quiet journalist for a bird-watchers' magazine. You, on the other hand, are the cop that could send me up the river."

"Well, we'll just stay here until they go away," Delaney said seductively as he moved closer to Rachel, who still had her back to the wall. "This will be our little secret."

"What are you doing?" she shrieked as his hand slipped through the folds of the blanket she had wrapped around her body and captured a bare breast.

"I'm coming up with something for us to do until they go away," he murmured against her ear.

Rachel shoved him aside. "Be serious, Del. They're not going to go away that fast."

"We're not in any rush. We don't have to catch a train to New York for hours. And that's assuming Mendez can get his hands on Thomas today."

"You'll have to get dressed and go out there," Rachel insisted. "Talk to them."

"Talk to them?"

"Yes, tell them . . . tell them something. Otherwise they could picket out here all day."

Delaney didn't look inspired.

"I know," Rachel said. "Tell them you're working on a new lead. Tell them that I'm no longer the prime suspect. Tell them anything that will make them go away."

"All right. I'll tell them something," Delaney mumbled. "But I'd much prefer—"

Rachel swatted away his hand as he went to make another grab for her. "Please get dressed and get out there, Del."

Delaney reluctantly backed off. As he passed the window, his gaze lit on another familiar face. "Your niece just rode up. Doesn't that kid ever go to school?"

"Skye? Oh, no." She hurried over to the phone by the side of the bed.

"Who are you calling?"

"Kate. If Skye's out there, that means Kate's probably awake already. What's she going to think when she realizes I'm not there?"

Delaney threw on some clothes while Rachel dialed Kate's number. Kate answered on the first ring. Rachel barely got to say, "Hello," before Kate started giving her the third degree.

"Take it easy, Kate. I'm fine. I'm with Del-aney. I remembered something earlier this morning—" she omitted that it was precisely six hours earlier "—and so I came right over here—"

"Remembered what?" Kate demanded.

"Very possibly," Rachel said conspiratorially, "the name of the man who murdered Nelson. Or at least the man who arranged for Nelson's murder. A big shot in the mob."

"You really think he's the one?" Kate asked excitedly.

Rachel hesitated. "Well . . . it's a lead. There's a . . . connection."

"What's Delaney going to do?"

"He's having the mobster brought in for questioning. Actually, I'm going into New York with him while he questions the suspect himself."

The picketers were getting restless. They began to chant.

"What am I hearing over there?" Kate asked.

Rachel sighed. "It seems Dad and Mellie and a few of the good folks of Pittsville have decided to make a ... sort of formal protest. Didn't you tell Dad that Delaney's already on my side? That he's trying to clear my name?"

"I did call him from my office last night and I was about to give him the latest update, but then my ex-mother-in-law showed up, in a complete tizzy, demanding to know how I was going to run a television station and cope with a sister who was a possible felon at the same time."

"She called me a felon?" Rachel said indignantly.

"A *possible* felon," Kate corrected. "Don't let it get to you. She's called me a lot worse. Anyway, she's only looking for any opportunity she can get to stick her two cents in. She spent forty minutes complaining about the new shopping show. Called it undignified and accused me of pandering to the good people of Pittsville's baser instincts. Wait until she sees Ben Sandler's next 'Pittsville Patter' show. He's interviewing the town's first cross-dresser. And his designer."

Rachel laughed. "I'll have to tune in, but right now I've got to go lay low until Delaney clears out our vocal protesters. If they know I'm here, they may get...the wrong idea."

"The wrong idea, huh? Just how early did you get to Delaney's place, Rachel?" Kate asked suspiciously.

"I've got to go," Rachel said, ducking the question. "Speak to you soon."

DELANEY'S APPEARANCE outside his front door was met with vociferous boos and hisses. Rachel, crouched down below the windowsill, was sure she could distinguish her father's hisses from everyone else's.

"Now listen, folks!" Delaney shouted. "As things stand right now, Rachel Hart is not being charged with jaywalking much less murder, so you can all calm down. The case is under investigation, and because Rachel was a . . . was close to the murder victim, naturally—"

"Naturally, nothing," came a familiar voice in the crowd. Rachel peeked over the sill to see her father stride up to Delaney. She prayed her dad wouldn't get it into his head to take a swing at him. And then she prayed that if he did, Delaney wouldn't retaliate.

"I know you're upset, Mr. Hart," Delaney said in a placating tone.

Leo Hart was practically nose to nose with Delaney. "You bet I'm upset, you lily-livered coward. Sneaking your way into my daughter's life under false pretenses, preying on an innocent young woman instead of using your time to get out there and find the real murderer."

"You don't just go out and find a murderer, Mr. Hart. I'm here because I'm hoping your daughter—"

"He's hoping to pin the murder on her, is what he's hoping!" another protester shouted angrily.

Rachel shook her head wearily, recognizing her niece's voice. Never was a Hart who didn't want to get into the act.

"I wouldn't trust a cop—especially a New York City cop," Skye declared, "as far as I could throw him."

Mellie Oberchon wildly waved her placard that read FREE RACHEL, beaning several of the other protesters with it. "This is a free country," she cried out. "Where someone's innocent until they're proven guilty!"

She made her way up front to stand beside Leo. "My daughter, Frannie, had this apartment in Oakland, California, and when she moved out her landlord charged her with having made these gouges in the Formica counters in the kitchen. Well, those gouges were there when Gretchen moved in and he knew it, but he thought he could prey on an innocent young thing, too. Only Gretchen was dating this very nice man, Allan Jefferson—or was it Jefferson Allan? Anyway, that's beside the point."

Delaney could only stare at her in wonder, the point, if there was one, completely lost on him.

"Whatever his name was," Mellie said, "he was a lawyer. And he cleverly told Gretchen to contact the former tenant of the apartment, who confirmed that not only were those gouges in the counter there when Gretchen moved in, but they were also there when she'd moved in. The point being," Mellie added, wagging her finger at Delaney, "don't think you can pin a bum rap, as they say on all those police shows on TV, on Rachel. You can't get away with it."

"I'm trying to tell you," Delaney said, his patience starting to wear thin. "Nobody's accusing Rachel of any crime." Yet! "Right now, you could say she's more a . . . material witness."

Ben Sandler, who wasn't carrying any placard, but who'd come out to the old Seymour place to cover the story, darted over to Delaney, with his cameraman, Joe Evans, a short, squat fellow in his late twenties, close on his heels, video camera at the ready.

Delaney raised his eyes skyward. This was all he needed. Talk about having his cover blown. Now he was going to find himself on the local news. And what if the story got picked up by AP, or by CNN or one of the other networks? Mendez would have his head for claiming that their prime suspect had just been made a prime witness.

"You mean Rachel saw the murderer?" Ben asked excitedly. "She can identify him? Is she being put under police protection? Who is it? Can you reveal the name? Can you give us anything?"

"Hold it!" Delaney shouted, trying to wave away the cameraman to no avail. "Now you're jumping the gun. When I said Rachel was a material witness, I only meant it in the broadest sense."

"Did she or didn't she witness the murder?" Ben persisted.

"No, not exactly..." Delaney started to say, when Rachel suddenly appeared at the front door.

"That's not true," she declared dramatically. "I did see the murderer."

Delaney did a double take. What was she doing there? What the hell was she saying?

Ben quickly nudged Joe to get Rachel on tape.

Rachel's unexpected appearance, coupled with her stunning announcement, brought instant silence to the protesters.

Rachel's gaze fell on her father who appeared half bewildered, half wary. "What were you doing in there, Rachel?" he demanded.

"I beat you all here by a few minutes," she lied, hoping she could pull it off as well as her "sales rep." "Delaney and I are working together on the investigation. I came over here so we could . . . get started early."

Out of the corner of her eye, she could see Delaney's faint smile. Oh, they'd gotten started early, all right. She quickly averted her gaze so he wasn't even in her peripheral vision. "In fact," she added, "we're going into New York City this very day to—"

Delaney grabbed her arm and pulled her back toward the house. "Can I have a word with you, Rachel?" he asked tightly.

Rachel flashed a smile to the crowd. "Be right back, folks. A little conference. Like I said, we're working together. . . ."

He yanked her through the door, cutting off the rest of her sentence. As soon as he got her inside, he slammed the door shut. "Do you mind telling me what's going on here?" he demanded. "I thought the whole point of my going out there was to protect your virtue. And what do you mean, you saw the murderer? *Did* you see the murderer?"

"No, of course I didn't see the murderer," Rachel said impatiently. "Do you think I'd keep something like that from you? Do you think I'm nuts?"

"Yes," he said succinctly.

"You started it," Rachel said blithely. "You told them I was a material witness. So I thought to myself, wait a minute. This might be just the ticket to smoke out the real killer. Let's say it is this John Thomas—"

"Rachel . . ."

"Okay, or say it isn't. Say it's somebody else. Maybe the guy in the blue sedan. Maybe . . . who knows? The point is . . ."

"Now you're starting to sound like your father's girlfriend."

"Pay attention here, Delaney. We have very little to go on, right?"

"Right," he said reluctantly.

"Nine will get you ten this Thomas character's got an alibi. Even if he were responsible, he wouldn't do the foul deed himself. He'd get a henchman to do it. So you question Thomas. So you get nowhere. So we're back to square one. And I'm right in the middle of that square with a noose hanging around my neck."

"We have to start somewhere. Tracking down a murderer takes time, Rachel."

"But time isn't on my side. We've got to step things up. We've got to get the killer nervous, force his hand."

Delaney gazed at her warily.

"What better way," she hurried on, "than for Nelson's murderer to think I saw him? Or her? And if he or she thinks I can identify him or her, what do you think he or she is going to do? I'll tell you what he or she is going to do. Come after me. Try to silence me before I finger . . ."

"Him or her?" Delaney said, deadpan.

"Exactly," Rachel replied. "You see it in the movies all the time."

Delaney's features darkened. "Yeah. Well, in the movies," he barked, "the heroine who's the sitting duck can't get killed by the real murderer, whoever he or she might be, or the audience would riot and demand their money back. They want a happy ending. They want the bad guy caught and the good gal to win out. Then the audience feels like they got their money's worth."

Rachel could see where he was going with his argument, but he went there anyway.

"In real life, there is no audience, Rachel. There is no guarantee of a happy ending. You set yourself up and something terrible could happen to you." He took in a ragged breath. "And I don't want to see that happen."

Rachel put her finger to his lips. "I guess you'll have to stick real close to me then and make sure nothing does happen."

He grabbed hold of her wrist. "I want you to go out there this minute and tell them all—especially Sandler—that you didn't see the murderer."

"You want me to admit I lied?"

"Yes," he said without hesitation.

"Why wouldn't they just think I was lying now? How would they know what to believe?" A predicament Rachel herself was all too familiar with.

"I'll back you up," Delaney said. "I'll explain that you just got a little carried away...." As he spoke he started to open the door, but Rachel put her hand against it.

"No, I can't do it, Del."

"Rachel, I don't think you realize—"

"I realize that if we don't do something drastic and do it fast, I could be sitting behind bars before my baby is even born. Right now, whoever killed Nelson is sitting pretty. I'm the perfect candidate for my ex-lover's murder. I had means, motive, and opportunity. Except for the killer, I was the last person to see Nelson alive. Everyone here in Pittsville may be convinced of my innocence, but you know as well as I do that back in New York I'm not only the star suspect, but probably the only suspect. Am I wrong, Del?"

He may not have squirmed visibly, but he was squirming inwardly. "No," he said quietly. "You're not wrong."

"My plan could work, couldn't it?" she coaxed.

"Rachel . . ."

"Couldn't it?" Her voice lowered a notch. "And if it did work and we smoked the real killer out, you'd finally be convinced—"

"About that, Rachel . . ."

"Beyond a shadow of a doubt. That's the way I want it," she insisted. "Making love doesn't change the facts, Del. I could have killed Nelson. You have no way of knowing for sure that I didn't, unless we catch the guy or the gal who did."

"What if . . . ?" He hesitated.

"What if what?" she asked.

He leveled his gaze on her. "What if it doesn't work? What if no one makes a move on you?"

Rachel shut her eyes for a moment. "You mean, what if I'm guilty and just playing for time?" She opened her eyes and met his gaze. "Or sympathy?"

He reached out and took hold of her. "No. I mean, the real killer might be shrewd enough to think you're bluffing."

"I don't buy it. It's too risky. I think we just might see that guy in the blue sedan show up again. Or someone else. It might even be—" She stopped, realizing she never had told Delaney about that love note she'd found in Nelson's apartment.

"Suzanne?"

Rachel blinked several times in surprise. "You know about Suzanne?"

"We found this letter."

Rachel nodded. "I found it, too."

Delaney didn't say anything.

Rachel knew what he was thinking. "Another motive for my killing Nelson, right?"

"How did you feel when you read it?" he asked softly.

Rachel looked away, not focusing on anything in particular. "Upset. Angry. Dumb."

"Dumb?"

"Kate and Julie say I have lousy instincts when it comes to men."

"Is that what you think?"

Rachel focused back on Del. She looked at him for several moments without answering. There was still that wistful longing in his eyes. "I hope not always," she murmured.

Her answer made him feel sad. He wanted to win Rachel's complete trust. Just as she wanted to have his complete trust. That wasn't going to happen until Nelson's murderer was behind bars. He knew then that he was no longer doubting Rachel's innocence. He also knew that his belief wouldn't be enough to save her.

"Do you know this Suzanne?" he asked.

"No. I never knew she existed until I read that letter."

"Is that why you left him? Because you realized he was cheating on you?"

"Only one of the reasons. I was upset and angry when I realized he was cheating on me, but I wasn't devastated. I guess the big thing I discovered when I uncovered the truth about Nelson was that I wasn't devastated by any of it. I think I loved the idea of being in love with Nelson rather than actually ever loving him. Something was always missing, but I could never put my finger on it. Maybe Nelson sensed that, on some level. Maybe that's why he and this Suzanne..." She shrugged. "It doesn't matter now."

Delaney wasn't so sure. "Her full name's Suzanne English. She lives in Philadelphia. She's a ... an exotic dancer."

Rachel looked at him blankly, then the light dawned. "You mean a stripper?"

"Well...yes. A stripper, unfortunately, with a pretty ironclad alibi for the night of Nelson's murder. She was ... doing her act at the time in a Philly club."

"Alibis. Everyone has an alibi but me," Rachel said glumly.

"We don't know that for sure, yet. There's still Thomas," Delaney responded, trying to sound upbeat but not succeeding.

Rachel gripped his sleeve. "My plan is our best shot. Maybe our only shot. It could work, Del. You know it could."

"Yes, it could work," he said reluctantly. "And you could also get yourself—"

This time she stopped him from finishing the sentence with a torrid, openmouthed kiss. It was a very effective silencer.

Just as their lips and tongues were getting happily reacquainted, the front door opened.

"I thought so."

Rachel and Delaney jumped apart at Leo Hart's dry observation.

"It isn't what you think," she muttered inanely.

"How do you know what I think?" her father replied, closing the door behind him.

"What *do* you think?" Delaney asked.

Leo mulled the question over for a few moments. "I think my daughter here takes after her mother, may she rest in peace."

Delaney glanced at Rachel, who stood there looking modestly chagrined and saying nothing. Delaney switched his gaze to her father.

"Meaning?" he asked.

"Meaning," Leo said, "that she's got this irrepressible spirit that can lead her into a mess of trouble. And sometimes into the arms of the wrong man."

"Dad..." Rachel began to protest, but Leo waved her off.

"Before Christina and I were married she got herself involved with a man who turned out to be a notorious gambler. Chrissie was completely in the dark until one of her girlfriends told her she'd seen him at the race-track, bragging to his companion how he was on a real winning streak." He lowered his head, peering up at Rachel. "His companion, by the way, being a curvy blond vixen by the name of Gloria, if I remember the story correctly."

Rachel squinted at her dad. "I never heard that story before."

Leo shrugged. "No reason you should have. Before."

"And after this gambler, you two hooked up?" Delaney asked.

Leo nodded.

"So," Rachel declared, "she didn't always make the wrong choice when it came to men."

Leo merely smiled at the pair of them.

Rachel and Delaney darted awkward glances at each other, then both of them stared down at the floor. The phone rang. Delaney dashed off for it, grateful for the distraction.

"That's probably Delaney's chief. At Homicide," Rachel muttered.

"What's this about you having seen the murderer?" her father asked solemnly.

"Well, I *may* have seen him. Outside the building that night." She'd never mastered the art of lying well. Especially to her father.

Leo shook his head. "Do you think I don't know what you're trying to cook up here, Rachel? Was this his idea?" He motioned in the direction Delaney had headed.

"No," Rachel said. "It was my idea."

"This is just like something your mother would pull. Or try to."

"It's the only way I can see to clear myself. Delaney's strongly against it."

Leo raised a salt-and-pepper eyebrow. "I suppose he was trying to talk you out of it when I came in."

Rachel blushed. "You mean . . . the kiss?"

A faint smile curved his lips. "No. Given how much you are like your mother, my guess is that was you *talking* him into it after he gave his best shot at getting you to change your mind."

Rachel smiled back. "He's a terrific guy, Dad."

"Terrific?" he echoed. "Is that so?"

Rachel knew what her father was thinking. "Okay," she said. "I admit I made a mistake with Nelson. Just like Mom made a mistake with that gambler. She got it right, though, when she chose you. I'm bound to get it right one of these days. Who knows? This could be the day." Then, after a pause, she added, "Or maybe not. Just because Del's terrific doesn't mean I expect anything." Which was saying a mouthful for a woman who, heretofore, had always expected too much when it came to love. Love. Was that what that funny feeling inside her was all about? And here she'd been thinking it was hunger pangs. Well, in a way it was hunger pangs. But it wasn't breakfast she was craving. It was Delaney Parker.

"I'll tell you one thing, Rachel."

She gave her father a curious look. "What's that?"

"I believe that cop in there would take a bullet for you if it came down to it—which I hope to God it doesn't." He paused for a moment, his gaze turning melancholy. "But marry you? That, I'm not so sure of."

Rachel swallowed hard. "Marriage? Who said anything about marriage? I told you . . . I don't expect anything from Delaney. I mean, let's face it. I'm not exactly a star candidate for marriage at the moment. I've got a couple of things that you wouldn't say are in my favor, if you know what I mean."

She knew her dad probably did know what she meant, but she spelled it out anyway. "I'm pregnant with another man's child. A man who turned out to be a mobster. And then went and turned up dead in our kitchen. And I'm the star suspect in his murder. I may never have to worry about getting married. To Delaney or the man in the moon. Unless either of them was willing to have our wedding ceremony held in a prison chapel. And wouldn't mind having to skip the honeymoon. Or our first twenty-five or so anniversaries. Or—" She flung her arms out in outrage, despair and frustration, only to make contact with something solid—Delaney's chest.

Oh God, she thought. How long had he been standing there?

There was an awkward silence broken finally by a knock on the door. It was Mellie, who gave them all an anxious look as she stepped inside the vestibule, which was now quite crowded. "Will there be any more statements to the media? Ben wants to know."

Delaney scowled. "No. No more statements. Everyone can just go on home."

"Oh, they have," Mellie said. "There's only Skye, Ben and little Joey Evans out there." She squinted at Rachel. "You've certainly set everyone abuzzing. Just imagine. Seeing the murderer. I remember, once, my good friend Edith Neiman, who moved to the Poconos to live with her daughter after her husband, Harry, passed away a few years back, witnessed a crime. She spied some strange man breaking into the house right across the street from her. Can you imagine?"

The question was purely rhetorical and Mellie went right on with her story. "He pulled open a window right there at the front of the house and climbed in, just as bold as you please. Right in broad daylight. Well, Edith imagined he'd cased the neighborhood already, as they say, and knew that just about everyone on the street worked, including Edith. Well, she didn't exactly work, but she did volunteer at the hospital for several hours each day. However, as she told us all at mah-jongg a few days later, on that particular day she had a cold and didn't want to risk the patients catching it, so she'd stayed home. She was sitting by the window, having some tea, when she looked out and saw the break-in. Naturally, she grabbed the phone immediately and called the police. After she hung up with them she phoned her daughter and talked with her until the police arrived on the scene."

She paused dramatically.

Her three listeners waited expectantly for her to go on.

Mellie's brown eyes widened. "They caught him red-handed. Well, *wet*-handed anyway," she said with a girlish giggle. "It turned out he was a window washer. The Merchants, who'd bought the house about a month earlier, had hired him and he was busy scrubbing away at the inside panes of glass when the two policemen jumped out of the cruiser, guns pointed."

Rachel and Delaney gave each other a look. Leo merely smiled.

Mellie sighed. "Edith had them in for tea and sandwiches."

"The cops?" Rachel asked.

"And the window washer, who'd had quite a fright," Mellie said. "Edith thought it was the least she could do. And the whole mah-jongg group ended up hiring Mr. Whitman to do our windows that spring." She smiled. "He was very good."

"I have no doubt of it," Leo said sweetly.

"In the end, it all worked out fine," Mellie concluded with a smile. Her smile lingered on Rachel as she added, "It usually does."

Delaney was trying to decipher how Mellie's story pertained to Rachel's predicament when he remembered the phone call.

"I almost forgot. That was Mendez on the phone," he told Rachel. "Thomas will be at the station by two. We could go into the city early and you can go over some of the statements we've collected from a few friends and acquaintances of Lang's," he suggested.

"Good idea," Rachel said.

They were both on the same wavelength, wanting to get away before Mellie Oberchon came up with another one of her stories.

"You better stop for some breakfast first," Mellie said, observing Rachel closely. "You look pale. Don't forget you're eating for two now."

Rachel nodded at the older woman, feeling Delaney's gaze on her. "No. I won't forget. We'll get something to eat at Ralph's Café before we get on the train."

Leo caught hold of his daughter's arm. "You be careful now. You don't want to go jumping from the frying pan into the fire."

Rachel nodded dutifully. Good, fatherly advice. Unfortunately, a little late in the coming.

April 10

To paraphrase *Hamlet*—which my English teacher, Mrs. Walters, is making us read. Ugh!—"Did she or didn't she?" Aunt Rachel, that is. Did she or didn't she see the killer?

I've had my suspicions all along. Still, if Aunt Rachel did see the killer, why didn't she say so right away? Maybe she was just scared. Who wouldn't be scared? Witnesses to murders sometimes get murdered themselves. Oh my God . . .

So, why come forward now? That's easy enough to figure out. She's got this big hunk of a cop to protect her. That's why.

On the other hand she could be lying—even the best of us tell a fib now and then! It could just have popped into her head to say that so all of us protesting her innocence out there on Delaney's front lawn would be so caught up in her startling announcement that we wouldn't be wondering what she was doing there in his house at that hour of the morning. Or wondering how long she'd been there. Everyone around here may think I'm a child, but I know plenty more about plenty of stuff than they think I know.

What's worrying me is, even if Aunt Rachel was lying and can't identify Nelson's murderer, Nelson's murderer won't know that. Aunt Rachel's jumped from the frying pan right into the fire, as my Grandpa Leo would say.

8

JONATHAN THOMAS II arrived at Manhattan's Forty-fifth Precinct at precisely two o'clock in the afternoon. He was a tall, tanned, athletically built man dressed in a meticulously cut blue suit, but instead of a businessman's starched white or pale blue shirt and classic tie, he wore a black silk T-shirt under the jacket. His hair was dark. He wore it long but very tidy, pulled straight back from his angular face and tied at the nape of his neck with a leather thong. His cordovan penny loafers were buffed to a warm sheen, but he wore them without socks. He also sported a pair of Armani sunglasses. The forty-seven-year-old head of Delta Records was, in a word, hip.

Accompanying the record mogul was his lawyer, Avery Bramson, a dapper gray-haired man who was dressed in more traditional business garb. Mendez nodded to the pair as they entered his office.

"What's this about?" Bramson demanded without preamble.

Jonathan Thomas II seemed only mildly interested in hearing the answer. He stood near the door, an insolent smirk on his face, his arms folded across his chest, keeping the sunglasses on even though the room was dimly lit.

"Strictly routine," Mendez said laconically from behind his desk.

Bramson looked over at Delaney, who was leaning against the wall right behind Mendez, then he narrowed his gaze back on the homicide chief. "What kind of a routine are we talking about?"

"We have reason to believe," Mendez said, "that Mr. Thomas here had some business dealings with a man whose murder we're currently investigating. We'd like to ask Mr. Thomas a few questions...."

Bramson's eyes darted to his client, then swung back to Mendez. "What man?"

"Nelson Lang."

"Never heard of him," Thomas drawled.

Bramson didn't look pleased. "Leave this to me, Mr. Thomas."

"We're within our rights to question your client," Mendez said.

Bramson opened his mouth to argue, but Thomas, who'd swaggered over to a seat, interrupted. "Go on and ask. I won't have any answers since I never heard of the guy."

The phone rang. Delaney leaned forward and got it. He listened for a few seconds, then hung up.

His gaze fell on Thomas. "You ever dine at Roberto's on West Fifty-fourth Street, John?"

An edginess overrode the record mogul's cocky expression. "What the hell . . . ?" He sprang up from his chair and yanked off his sunglasses, his eyes sweeping the small office. He zeroed in on the large rectangular mirror on the back wall. "You got someone in there spying on me? Who is it? That slimy maître d' who thinks he's God's gift to the human race? Okay, sure. I've eaten at Roberto's a couple of times. Since when is that a crime?"

RACHEL FELT A FLASH of alarm when Thomas stared straight into the mirror. They were practically eye to eye. She relaxed a little when he mentioned the maître d'.

"Very good, Miss Hart."

Rachel spun around at the sound of the voice at the door. "Mr. Kelso."

He gave her a perfunctory smile as he stepped into the small, unadorned observation room and shut the door.

"Roberto's was Nelson's favorite restaurant. Or at least, it was one of the few places he ever took me to," she said, her gaze drifting back to the one-way mirror. "As soon as I saw Thomas in there, I remembered seeing him at Roberto's."

Kelso adjusted the knot in his gray-and-blue striped tie, then put his hands in the pockets of his gray serge jacket. "How often did you see Thomas at Roberto's?"

Rachel thought for a moment. "A few times."

"Did Lang and Thomas have any exchanges there? Did you ever see them talk to each other, notice if they passed anything between them?"

"Well . . . no."

"Was Thomas there alone or with other people? Men? Women? If you looked through mug shots, do you think you could identify any of his dining companions?" He rattled off each question.

Rachel wished she'd been more observant. "I don't know. I guess I could try." She didn't sound too optimistic.

"Did Thomas ever come to Lang's apartment while you were there?"

"No. We never had guests."

"Didn't you think that was odd?"

"Not odd, but . . ."

"But what?"

"I did try to encourage Nelson to be more . . . outgoing. And less . . ." She paused, struggling for the right word. "Not exactly possessive, but it did feel like he wanted to keep our relationship in a separate little world." She laughed harshly. "Now I know why."

"You sound bitter."

Rachel stiffened. "You mean bitter enough to have stabbed him? No. Why would I need to kill him when I could just leave him? Which is exactly what I did."

Kelso nodded, his expression unreadable. Rachel, however, could read between the lines. She knew he thought she was guilty. How could she convince him . . . ?

And then something came to her. "I do remember that whenever we went out to a restaurant, Roberto's included, Nelson always went off to the men's room before he sat down at the table. I used to tease him sometimes about it, until he confided in me that he had a weak bladder. Then I felt bad and never mentioned it again."

"You're saying Thomas and Lang could have rendezvoused in the men's room?"

"Well . . . yes."

"You mean you saw Thomas go off to the men's room at the same time as your boyfriend on each occasion?"

"No, but—"

"On any occasion?"

"No, but I don't know that he didn't." She sighed. "It isn't much, is it?" she asked.

Kelso gave a little shrug.

Rachel could feel the noose start to tighten around her neck. She swallowed hard and keyed back in to the interrogation going on at the other side of the mirror. Maybe Del would get something out of Thomas that would get her off the hook.

"MY CLIENT HAS ALREADY told you," Bramson said tightly, "that he does not know Nelson Lang. The fact that the two men may both have dined at the same restaurant doesn't mean anything. On top of that, Mr. Thomas has an alibi for the night you say Mr. Lang was murdered. He was at his studio meeting with a new recording group." He glanced over at his client. "The Storm Troopers, right?"

"Right," Thomas confirmed cockily. "We got started around ten that night and didn't break up until five in the morning. We were ironing out a deal and there was quite a bit of haggling going on."

Bramson smiled smugly. "You can check with the rock group."

"Don't let them hear you call them 'rock' or they'll stone you," Thomas said with a smirk. "They're rhythm and blues." He turned to Delaney. "You into rhythm and blues, Parker?"

Delaney perched himself on the edge of the desk, directly in front of Thomas, who was once again slouched in a seat, his legs straight out and crossed at his bare ankles.

"I try to avoid the blues," Delaney said glibly.

Bramson rubbed his hands together. "Well, gentlemen, if there are no more questions—"

"Just one," Delaney said, stopping Bramson midsentence. "Something's got me stumped." His gaze was fixed on Thomas. "If you didn't know Nelson Lang, how is it that he kept this accounting of business dealings with you, John? All neatly recorded in a little black notebook?"

Thomas's legs jerked involuntarily. *Bingo*.

Thomas swung his head to the side, his eyes flashing on his lawyer. Bramson compressed his lips, a sign for his client to remain mute.

Delaney smiled blandly. "You can think about it for a while. That's all, for now." He snatched up a business card off the desk and flicked it at Thomas. "If you come up with any answers, you can reach us at this number." He sauntered over to the door and opened it. "See you again, John."

RACHEL COULDN'T BELIEVE what she was seeing. That was it? That was all Delaney was going to say? Couldn't he see that he was just getting to Thomas? The instant he'd mentioned Nelson's notebook, Thomas had gone practically white. Delaney had him. Why didn't he come down harder on him? Harder? That was a laugh. He'd treated Thomas with kid gloves. If that was Delaney's idea of a third degree, she was a goner.

She looked over to see what Kelso's reaction was, but the FBI agent was gone. He'd slipped out of the room as quietly as he'd slipped in.

Kelso had joined Delaney and Mendez for a brief postmortem in Mendez's private office.

"If you had that notebook . . ." the chief was saying.

Delaney gave Mendez a rueful grimace. "Yeah. If."

"We know one thing," Kelso said. "Thomas doesn't have the notebook or he wouldn't have looked so worried."

"Too bad the Hart woman can't remember any other names in that book," Mendez said.

Kelso shrugged. "Can't or doesn't want to."

Delaney glared at him.

Kelso smiled. "Okay, okay, don't blow my head off. It's just a thought."

Delaney leaned forward. "What it tells me is that Thomas, or someone besides Thomas, was worried enough about incriminating evidence to send a hood out to reclaim that notebook."

"Well, if that somebody, whoever he is, got it," Mendez replied, "it's not likely your hood will resurface."

"I'm not so sure," Delaney muttered. If Rachel's plan worked, he might resurface in spades.

"Even if we had that notebook in hand," Kelso said, "all it would actually prove is that Lang had business dealings with some questionable characters. It doesn't mean one of them iced him."

"It doesn't mean one of them didn't," Delaney countered.

"We'll keep a watch on Thomas," Mendez said, but he didn't sound overly optimistic.

Kelso nodded. "We're interested in him, as well. We've known for years that he's tied to organized crime, but we've never been able to prove it. Nailing Thomas would be a real feather in my cap. You did get him nervous, Delaney. And nervous people tend to make dumb mistakes. Nice work."

Mendez nodded grudgingly. He wasn't big on compliments. "If Thomas's alibi checks out—and something tells me it will—seems to me we're back where we started as far as Lang's murder goes." He tapped a pencil on his desk. "We've got her right here, Delaney. Why not save yourself some grief and have us book her now?"

"You said one week," Delaney reminded tightly.

Mendez and Kelso made eye contact.

"Look," Delaney said, his voice thick with frustration. "Anyone could have come up to that apartment within minutes of Rachel's departure. Since security is pretty tight in the building, odds are it was someone Lang knew and let in. Someone he did business with. Someone who wanted to terminate the partnership."

"It's a nice theory," Kelso observed. "But where's the proof?"

"It's not proof," Delaney said, "but don't you think it's interesting that the apartment was clean except for that love letter? Whoever stabbed Lang must have gone through the place and retrieved any incriminating documents."

"Like that notebook?" Kelso remarked nonchalantly.

"That notebook got overlooked. Lang had it stuck in a zippered compartment of a suitcase. When Rachel took off, she happened to use that suitcase and it wasn't until she'd unpacked at her sister's house that she found it." Even as he was talking, he knew the story sounded weak. He also believed it was the truth.

"Why didn't she report her find to us?" Mendez asked.

"She didn't know that it was anything. She had more pressing problems on her mind. She wanted to get on with her life."

Kelso rubbed his jaw. "Is this multiple choice, Delaney?"

"No. And it's not a joke, either," he snapped. "You guys are just looking for an easy way out."

Mendez busied himself with a thread on his shirtsleeve. "I don't really see as how you're gonna pull this rabbit out of a hat by the end of the week, Delaney."

"And what happens if time runs out and you come up empty-handed? What happens if she bolts? That would leave us all with egg on our faces," Kelso said, grabbing a handful of jelly beans from a glass candy dish on Mendez's desk. He checked them out, returning all the green ones. Satisfied, he popped the rest into his mouth at once.

Delaney, whose stomach had been acting up lately, looked on with disgust. "Don't you ever worry about cavities?"

Kelso swallowed, then grinned widely. "False teeth."

Mendez chuckled.

Delaney threw up his hands. "I've got to go."

When he got to the door, he stopped and turned back to face the two men. "A lot can happen in a week." Nobody knew that better than him.

RACHEL WAS FUMING silently as she sat across from Delaney at a white-linen covered table in a small, modest French bistro near the precinct. What made her even angrier was the nonchalant way Delaney was behaving.

Feeling her eyes on him, Delaney looked up from his plate, after popping a piece of chicken into his mouth. His stomach was still a bit queasy, but he figured it was because he hadn't eaten much that day. A little fuel, and he'd be good as new.

"Aren't you hungry?" he asked.

"No," she said sharply, her own plate of poached salmon with hollandaise sauce untouched. "And don't remind me that I'm eating for two."

"I didn't think you needed any reminding," Delaney said quietly, as he carved off another succulent morsel of chicken and deposited it into his mouth.

She watched him chew for several moments, then finally she couldn't take it anymore. "What happened back there, Delaney?"

He didn't miss her switch from Del to Delaney. "It went real well," he said.

Rachel couldn't believe her ears. "Real well? If that little exchange with Thomas went real well, I'd hate to see what you'd call real poor. Why did you stop just when you had him starting to sweat?"

Delaney rested his fork on his plate. "Because I wanted him to sweat some more. I wanted him to stew in his sweat for a while. And I didn't want to give my hand away."

"What hand?" Rachel asked sardonically.

Delaney smiled. "Exactly. I was bluffing. We can't produce that notebook as material evidence. We're holding anything but a winning hand here, Rachel. If I'd tried to push Thomas, I'd have given that away, and he could have gone off feeling like he'd not only won the hand but the whole game."

Rachel thought it over. Then she looked across at Delaney and nodded slowly. "You really are good at what you do, aren't you?"

He smiled. "I like to think so. I like it better, thinking that you think so."

Rachel was touched, but she was also still preoccupied by the prospect of a jail sentence. "What does Mendez think? Is he . . . optimistic?"

Delaney speared an asparagus. "Well . . . I wouldn't go that far."

"How far would you go?" she pressed.

"He's sort of taking a 'Let's wait and see' attitude." Delaney didn't add that Mendez was only willing to "wait and see" for another six days. Or that he'd have his head on a platter if Rachel took it into her head at any point to go on the lam.

"I don't think our Mr. Kelso from the FBI was too impressed," Rachel said, her anger replaced by a mounting sense of doom. She forced herself to eat a little of the salmon. Dr. Moss had made a big point of her needing to eat a lot of protein. One mouthful, though, and she felt a wave of nausea rise up from her stomach to the back of her throat.

"Are you okay?" Delaney asked. Before she could answer, he said, "No, of course you're not okay. You're as white as the tablecloth."

Rachel sprang up. "I'll be . . . right back."

Delaney watched her hurry off through the opening leading to the bar and the rest rooms beyond. He shook his head wearily. Nothing about this case had gone as planned. Not only did he believe the woman he was investigating for murder was innocent, he was pretty damn sure he was falling in love with her. Or something close enough to love to give him indigestion. Sympathy pangs, maybe? This was really getting serious.

He tried another bite of chicken. It was tepid and tasted like rubber now. He reached across the table and sampled some of Rachel's salmon. It didn't taste much better.

He looked off toward the entrance to the bar. Where was Rachel? What was taking her so long? What if she'd passed out in the ladies' room? What if she was in there, having a miscarriage?

He bolted up from his seat and raced across the dining area only to collide with Rachel as he turned the corner leading into the bar.

"Rachel, are you all right?" he asked anxiously. Her face was flushed and she grabbed onto him.

"Wait till you see," she said, pulling him by the sleeve over to the bar. She pointed to the TV. The evening news was on CNN.

The newscaster was breaking the story that Rachel Hart, fiancée of Nelson Lang, had announced that morning in her hometown of Pittsville, New York, that she was an eyewitness to Lang's murder. The actual taped footage of her announcement—courtesy of WPIT in Pittsville—flashed on the screen.

Rachel groaned. "Oh, I look awful."

The bartender, standing a few feet away, glanced over at her. Delaney spun her around before he got a good look at her, and hurriedly steered her back into the restaurant.

"You don't look happy," Rachel said. "This is what we wanted—"

"This is what *you* wanted," Delaney reminded her. "Are you going to eat any more of your dinner?"

Rachel shook her head. "I can't. I'll eat something later. I'm just too wired."

Delaney threw some money down on the table. "Let's get out of here."

They headed for Grand Central Station, a short walk from the restaurant. Delaney had to keep slowing down so Rachel could keep up with him. He didn't say anything.

"I wonder," Rachel said, "if John Thomas caught the news tonight."

"I wonder if he's got some of his boys waiting in the alley up ahead to grab you," Delaney muttered.

Rachel's gaze shot to the alley. Was Delaney trying to scare her? If he was, he was doing a pretty good job of it.

Her fear multiplied when Delaney switched to her right side—putting her closer to the curb and farther from the alley—as they got closer.

A car drove by. A blue sedan. Rachel gasped, clutching Delaney's arm.

Delaney shook his head. "It's not our friend. He ditched the blue car. He could be driving around in any make or model now," he told her soberly.

They made it past the alley without incident. They made it all the way to the train in one piece. Still, it wasn't as though Rachel could breathe a sigh of relief even as the train pulled out of the station. Someone could be lying in wait for her on board. Or back in Pittsville. She reminded herself that this was her doing. Her only chance to clear herself. *Or die trying.*

Delaney took hold of her hand; it was ice cold. And, if anything, it was uncomfortably warm and stuffy on the train. "You could make a statement retracting what you said about having witnessed the murder, Rachel."

"I'm scared," she said. "I admit it. But I'm also plenty scared of going to prison on a bum rap. I still think this is the only way."

He nodded, giving her a close scrutiny.

"I'm okay," she assured him, also hoping to assure herself.

"No, you're more than okay, Rachel."

"You mean I'm more than you bargained for."

He smiled. "That, too."

She rested her head on his shoulder right where it connected to his neck. A lovely spot. She closed her eyes as his hand stroked her hair. "That feels nice, Del," she murmured, snuggling in closer.

"Rachel, I think you should move in with me."

Her head sprang up. "What?"

Red blotches spotted his cheeks. "I don't think it's safe for you—or for your family—for you to stay at your sister's. Until this is over."

Now, matching red blotches popped up on Rachel's cheeks. "Oh. Right. I wasn't . . . thinking." Not about that, anyway.

Delaney fiddled with the nonexistent crease in his chinos. Maybe if he worked at it, he could create one. "I wish it were under . . . different circumstances." His voice took on a husky quality.

Rachel stared at a poster advertising baby food. A picture of a cherubic baby nestled contentedly in its mother's arms. No daddy in the picture. It figured. "Sure. I understand, Del. We're talking police protection, not proposition."

He cupped her chin, his gray-green eyes boring into her. "Rachel, nothing like this has ever happened to me before. I'd even been looking for it to happen lately, but I didn't really think, down in my gut, that it would. And now it has."

"What's happened, Del?" she asked hesitantly.

The usually self-contained Delaney Parker was suddenly tongue-tied. "I'm . . . crazy about you, Rachel. I . . ."

She drew his hand away from her face. "No. Don't, Del. Don't say anything more. It's all really hitting me now. I'm not someone you want to be crazy about. I'm the last woman in the world any man in his right mind should be crazy about. My life is crazy right now. It's bad enough I've forced you into this cat-and-mouse game with a killer. I'm not going to wreak havoc on your personal life, as well."

"It's too late, Rachel."

"No, it isn't. We just got a little carried away. If I hadn't shown up at your door last night, practically thrown myself at you—"

"It would only have been a matter of time before I threw myself at you," he interrupted. "And not much time at that. Even when I first saw your photo back in Lang's apartment, something switched on inside of me, Rachel. Then, meeting you, spending time with you... This is all new to me. I'm probably saying it all wrong."

Tears spilled over the rims of her eyes. "No, you're not saying it all wrong, Del. It's just that you shouldn't be saying it at all."

Anguish ripped through him, seeing the anguish on her face.

"I'm crazy about you, too," she confessed, swiping at her tears with the back of her hand.

Delaney started to smile.

"But it's impossible."

"No, it's not," he argued. "Sure, you're going through some tough times right now, but ..."

"Tough times? Delaney, face it. We haven't the foggiest clue who killed Nelson. Thomas could be one of dozens of suspects, none of whom I even know. Even if someone does try to make a move on me, it doesn't mean we'll nab him. How much longer before your chief issues a warrant for my arrest? Whether you admit it or not, he still thinks I'm guilty. And so does Kelso."

He took hold of her hands. "We'll take it one step at a time. The first step is, we stop at your sister's house as soon as we get back, you pack your bag and we head over to my place."

Rachel withdrew her hands. "The only way I'm willing to stay at your place—temporarily—is if we have an . . . understanding."

"Meaning?"

"Meaning one of us sleeps on the couch. Meaning no hanky-panky. Meaning this arrangement is strictly . . . professional."

"Is that really what you want, Rachel?"

"What I want?" she echoed raspily. "No, it's not what I want. I want to be in the clear. I'm having a baby in five and a half months. I want to be that baby's mother. I want to be there when she cries so I can wrap her in my arms and comfort her. I want to be there when she takes her first step, not dishing out slop in a prison cafeteria. I want to be free to fall in love. I want a lot of things that I can't have right now, Del. So, please don't make this any harder on me than it already is. Please," she beseeched.

Parallel furrows of pain, frustration and concession appeared between Del's eyes. "Okay, Rachel." He reached out for her hand, then thought better of it. "But I take the couch and I don't want any argument about it."

Rachel smiled gratefully. "Thanks, Del."

They rode in silence for about ten minutes before he turned to her. "If you change your mind, though, you'll let me know."

"I'll let you know," she whispered.

April 11

Big doings here in Pittsville. First Aunt Rachel's story of her being an eyewitness to Nelson's murder makes it to CNN. We all saw it. Mom and Aunt Julie are nervous wrecks. They think Aunt Rachel's a sitting duck.

Then Aunt Rachel came in last night and announced that she was moving in with Delaney! Oh, she made it sound like it was strictly for her safety and ours, but we all know the score. Not that I acted like I knew the score, or Mom would have sat me down for another one of her birds-and-bees lectures.

Aunt Julie was bummed that she had to catch a plane back to Washington this morning. She promised my mom that she'd do some further digging into Nelson's underworld activities and hopefully come up with some leads. She promised me that I could come visit her this summer. Then she said that I might be seeing her even sooner. At her wedding! She's pretty sure Jordan's going to pop the big question any day now, and Aunt Julie says she's not one for long engagements. I didn't tell her, but my guess is she's worried if she stays engaged for too long, Jordan might get cold feet. My mom thinks no man ever really *wants* to get married.

Okay, I'm saving the best for last. This afternoon when I got home from school, I found a note from mom reminding me to vacuum. I hate vacuuming, but then I don't drool with delight over doing the dishes or scrubbing the kitchen floor, either. I decided to do my homework first. Even a page of math problems is better than dragging a vacuum through the house. No sooner did I finish the last math problem—a real toughie—than I got a call from Alice, of all people. She'd seen Aunt Rachel on CNN and she was just dying to talk about it. I was real cool on the phone, but then she started saying how it was totally dumb of her to have made that stupid remark about the innocent ones usually being the ones who were guilty. "Dumb" and "stupid" in the same sentence. This was really something coming from Alice, who happens to be one of the smartest kids in school and knows it!

We ended up talking for close to an hour. Then, as soon as I hung up with Alice, I got a call from Mom saying that she had to stay at the station late and could I heat up some soup and make a sandwich for myself. I made baloney and cheese, but I skipped the soup.

I finally got around to the vacuuming after I ate. I almost didn't bother with Aunt Rachel's room, but then I could hear my mom saying, "Skye, if you're going to do something, do it right."

So, I not only vacuumed Aunt Rachel's room, I even decided to do a quick run over her closet floor.

And that's when I found what could be the clue that will break this whole case wide open!

At first I didn't think it was anything much. A folded piece of paper. It turned out to be something, all right. A letter—or at least the beginning of a letter. And what a beginning!

On the top of the paper, in embossed black letters, was written, "From the desk of Nelson Lang." It was dated March 9. March 9. That's just five days before Nelson was murdered. The letter began, "My dearest

S, This is so hard for me to tell you, but I'm afraid we have to stop seeing each other...."

Uh-oh, I just heard a funny squeaking sound from out in the hall, and Mom's not due home for another hour. It's probably nothing. On the other hand ...

I was going to wait until morning to show this letter to Aunt Rachel and Delaney, but I think I'll bike on down there right now....

9

"YOU'RE QUIET," Rachel said as she and Delaney sat together in Delaney's small, knotty-pine-paneled living room on their second evening of "domestic cohabitation."

It was a far cry from domestic "bliss." Delaney was not only quiet; he was also exhausted, and on edge. Not only was his couch lumpy, but he'd found sleep utterly elusive the night before, with Rachel bedded down right in the next room. All night long, he'd been consumed by lascivious fantasies, which were broken only by intermittent flashes of alarm at the slightest unexpected sound. Would Nelson's killer show up? Would there be an attempt on Rachel's life? Would he be quick enough to avert catastrophe? Would he ever get another decent night's sleep?

While Delaney pretended avid interest in a fishing magazine—he'd gone fishing once in his life, that summer he'd spent at that camp for underprivileged kids, and ended up with poison ivy—Rachel wandered over to the small pine bookshelf near the window and started thumbing through the paperback books left behind by a variety of past tenants. Someone had been a big fan of sci-fi. Rachel wasn't—although the idea of being transported to another planet had its appeal.

"Want to play cards?" Rachel asked, spying a deck on the bottom shelf of the bookcase. She was finding the silence unsettling. She found everything unsettling at the moment, especially being Delaney's platonic houseguest. But she'd set up the rules. Delaney was merely obliging. "I'm a whiz at hearts."

He looked up from the magazine he really wasn't reading. "How are you at poker?"

"Lousy."

He grinned. "Good. We'll play poker."

"What kind of poker?" she asked warily. But she was smiling.

Delaney's eyes sparkled.

Rachel pursed her lips as she sat down at the small pine table across from the couch. "We're doing it again," she said.

"What are we doing?"

"We're flirting."

"Is flirting taboo? I thought it was just making love—"

"Delaney."

"Okay, I'm sorry."

"No, I started it. I'm the one that should be sorry."

"Okay, so you're sorry."

Rachel sighed. "No, I'm not sorry. That's the problem."

"What are you saying, Rachel?"

She absently pulled out the deck of cards from the pack and began shuffling them. They flew all over the table. "I don't know what I'm saying. Or doing."

Delaney set his magazine aside and walked over to her. He came up behind her and placed his hands gently on the back of her neck.

Even as she let her head drop to give him better access, she knew she should be telling him to stop. The protest wouldn't come. What she really wanted to be saying was, *Oh, that feels so good. More. Give me more.*

She thought he must have read her mind because she suddenly felt the tip of his tongue trail from the nape of her neck right around to her ear. His warm, moist breath sent a ripple of longing clear through her. The best-laid plans . . .

He circled around until he was facing her. Without a word he drew her up from her chair. She could feel her insides turning to liquid.

As his mouth began its descent to hers, she told herself that rules were meant to be broken. Besides, if she did end up being carted off to "the big house," at least she'd have these magical moments to remember.

Her arms snaked around his neck and she smiled up at him. "Oh, Del . . ."

"Rachel, listen. I think there's someone prowling around outside," he whispered.

Rachel froze.

"Don't look panicked."

"Am I looking panicked?" she asked, not moving her lips.

He drew her closer, wrapping his arms around her. "Smile."

Rachel gave it her best shot, but it came off as more of a pained grimace. She was clinging to him. "What should we do?" she whispered against his ear.

"Pretend we're getting carried away by lust."

A minute ago it wouldn't have been pretend. Now lust had been replaced by terror.

"Stay calm," she muttered. "Stay calm."

"I am calm, Rachel," he murmured, stroking her back.

"I'm not talking to you."

He nuzzled her neck. "Are you scared?"

"No."

He could feel her trembling with fear. "Liar."

She tilted her head up. "Kiss me. Make it a good one."

"To be convincing?"

"No. Because it may be my last."

"It won't be your last. I promise. But I'll give it all I've got, anyway."

He delivered, as promised, a kiss so intense and passionate that under any other circumstances they would have both been goners. As it was, it was only part of the performance.

Delaney was the one who broke away. He led a shaky Rachel over to the lumpy floral print Early American couch and sat her down. She appreciated his assistance. She needed all the help she could get. As Delaney went around turning out the lights, Rachel tried to pretend they weren't being observed, all the while having to force herself not to sneak a glance out the window.

The room was nearly pitch-black, with only a sliver of a moon out that night. Rachel couldn't see anything at first and let out a little gasp when Delaney joined her on the couch.

It's only me. Relax," Delaney whispered.

"Relax? Oh, sure." She heard a faint click. "What's that?"

"It's okay. It's my gun."

Rachel shut her eyes. Her heart was pounding against her chest. "Why didn't you talk me out of this?"

"Very funny."

"You're not laughing."

"Neither are you."

"I may never laugh again." She put her hand to her stomach. Her baby might never get the chance to have a first laugh. What had possessed her to come up with this crazy scheme? She knew what: desperation.

Delaney put his arm around her. She snuggled against him for reassurance. "What's he waiting for?" she asked in a tense whisper.

That was when they both heard a rustling sound, followed by a muted cry.

Delaney sprang to his feet, gun in one hand, a flashlight he'd grabbed from the bookcase in the other.

"Stay put," he ordered, as he darted for the front door. Too scared to stay put, Rachel followed on his heels.

The front door flew open and Delaney leaped outside, flashing the light in the intruder's face. Startled, the intruder spun away from the brightness. "Make one more move," Delaney barked, "and I put a bullet right through your back."

The intruder froze. "Don't shoot. Please. It's only me."

Rachel, her expression incredulous, popped her head out the door. "Skye?"

Skye slowly turned to face them. "Yes."

Delaney muttered an assortment of curses under his breath.

"I'm sorry," Skye said, her voice shaky. "I didn't mean to freak you guys out. I needed to show you something, but when I checked at the window to make sure you were home . . . you two started kissing and all, and I didn't want to . . . interrupt anything. I was going to hang around out here until . . . for a while, only I stumbled on a rock and skinned my knee, which was why I cried out."

Rachel started to laugh.

"It isn't funny, Aunt Rachel. I think I'm bleeding."

"Oh, I'm not laughing at you, honey," Rachel said apologetically, hurrying over to her niece. "I'm just so relieved. We thought you were . . ."

Skye's eyes widened. "The murderer?"

"We'd better all go inside and check out your knee before gangrene sets in," Delaney said sardonically.

"Right," Rachel said, putting an arm around Skye. "Can you walk, honey? Would you like Delaney to carry you?"

"I would *not* like Delaney to carry me, thank you," Skye said sharply, marching into the house under her own steam.

Rachel grinned at Delaney. Delaney scowled, returning his gun to his waistband.

Once inside, Rachel told Skye to roll up her jeans so she could see the damage.

Skye did her own quick check. "No, it's okay. Really. It just kind of smarted for a minute. It's only a scrape. Anyway, my knee's not important. This, however, is," she said dramatically, pulling out her "clue" from her back pocket and handing it to Rachel.

Rachel gave the sheet a puzzled look as she unfolded it. Delaney came up behind her, reading over her shoulder.

My dearest S,

This is so hard for me to tell you, but I'm afraid we have to stop seeing each other. It was great while it lasted, but we both knew what we had wasn't really going to go anywhere. If you got the signals wrong, I'm sorry. . . .

It ended there.

Rachel looked over her shoulder at Delaney. "It's Nelson's handwriting."

She studied the salutation. "S. Suzanne?" Or did Nelson have a Sarah or a Sharon or a Samantha in the wings, as well?

"Where'd you find this?" Delaney asked Skye.

"At the bottom of my aunt's closet."

Rachel frowned. "It must have been in the suitcase. It could have fallen out of that notebook."

Delaney took the letter in hand. "Wonder why he didn't finish it."

"Maybe he didn't have the time," Rachel said. "Or this could have been a first draft. He could have rewritten it and sent that one off."

"It would be real helpful to know if 'S.' got it," Delaney said.

"Right," Skye piped in excitedly, forgetting all about her skinned knee. "Getting jilted is a perfect motive for murder."

Rachel and Delaney shared a look. Didn't they both know it?

The phone rang. Rachel answered it. It was Kate. "It's okay. Skye's fine. She's right here."

Delaney motioned Skye over to the phone.

Rachel rolled her eyes. "Your mom's fit to be tied."

Skye gave a sick smile as she took up the receiver. "Before you blow up at me, Mom, you should know that I may have just broken this case wide open."

"Oh really, Skye," Kate said wearily at the other end of the line. "You might have at least left me a note. I walk into the house, every light is on, the vacuum cleaner is sitting in the middle of the guest room—"

"I'm sorry, Mom. I didn't mean to scare you. The thing is I found this important clue and I thought I should get it right over to Delaney and Aunt Rachel. Anyway, I heard this noise and I guess I kind of freaked a little."

Delaney shot Skye a look. "You heard a noise? You didn't say anything about a noise."

Rachel clutched Delaney's shirtsleeve. "How would the murderer know I was here with you?"

"If Skye really did hear someone in the house, he knows now."

"I don't know if it was really anything," Skye was telling her mother. "I was a little jumpy being all alone in the house."

Delaney took the receiver from Skye. "Any sign of a break-in, Kate? Anything in the house disturbed?"

"Only me," Kate said dryly. "Could you please give Skye a lift back here? She can pick her bike up in the morning." She sighed. "Kids."

"Yeah," Delaney murmured, his gaze straying to Rachel's gently rounded stomach. "They're really something."

IT WAS A LITTLE past eleven at night. Delaney rolled over on the narrow couch, hoping that he'd have less trouble falling asleep on his stomach than on his back. No use. He was wide-awake.

And he knew what was keeping him awake; what was likely to keep him away all night. Rachel.

He got up, looked over at the closed door to the bedroom. Was she asleep? He padded over to the door, listened, then knocked lightly.

"Yes," Rachel answered the knock instantly.

"You still awake?"

"Yes."

"Can I come in for a sec?"

"Yes."

He cracked the door open. Rachel was sitting up in bed, the blanket pulled primly up to her neck. Still, the sight of her face alone was enough to do it. He felt instantly aroused.

"What's up?" she asked.

Delaney fought back a smile. If he told her, she'd send him marching. "I was thinking."

"Yes?"

"About that letter. About Suzanne."

"And?"

"What do you say we take a trip out to Philly tomorrow?"

The blanket slid down to Rachel's lap. She was wearing an oversize bright green Celtics T-shirt. She looked terrific.

Rachel was oblivious to how she looked or where Delaney's mind was drifting. "To see Suzanne? But her alibi?" She sank back wearily against her pillows and emitted a vocal sigh.

"Forget her alibi for a minute. We're talking motive, here. The way Mendez and Kelso see it, Suzanne was hot for Lang and they assume he was hot for her. That means she'd have no reason to want him dead. If, on the other hand, Lang did send her off a version of the letter we saw, it does give her a reason for doing him in." As he was talking, Delaney kept finding his gaze straying to Rachel's wild tangle of auburn curls which contrasted so sharply against the white pillowcase.

"The same reason it gives me," she reminded him. "And, unfortunately, I was at Nelson's apartment very near the time of his murder, whereas Suzanne was in Philadelphia, undulating on a runway, and taking off all her clothes in front of a roomful of men." She sighed. "I never thought I'd ever find myself wishing I could trade places with a stripper."

"Bet you'd be sensational," he said playfully.

"Oh, right. Especially now. I'd make a real splash with my big belly. . . ."

"You have a beautiful body, Rachel. It's going to get more beautiful with each passing month."

Rachel stared at him. "You really mean that, don't you?"

His smile was boyish and disarming. "I really mean it."

She reached her hand out from her lap. He took it, entwining his fingers with hers. They held on tightly.

Her free hand moved to her stomach. "I wish it was your baby." She was startled by her own admission. Not that she hadn't had the thought on a number of occasions lately, but to say it aloud . . . To say it to Delaney.

She shut her eyes. "Oh, Del, I'm sorry. I don't know what made me . . ."

He gathered her roughly in his arms. "Yes, you do. You're in love with me."

She opened her eyes. "I am?"

He smiled at her, stroking her hair back from her face with his fingers. "Yes."

Her lips trembled. "You're right."

"I love you, too, Rachel. I love that baby you're carrying inside you. That baby's a part of you. How could I help but love it?"

She pressed her head against his shoulder to hide her sudden rush of tears. Falling in love when her whole world was coming unglued. Talk about lousy timing.

He held her close, stroking her. "Hey, don't. Don't. It's going to work out." He tilted her head back, kissing away the tears that ran down her cheeks, tasting their saltiness on the tip of his tongue.

"I really think it's going to be almost as awful for you as it's going to be for me if you end up having to book me."

"I won't."

Her eyes narrowed. "You won't feel awful?"

He kissed her hard on the mouth—a kiss that he felt sealed his fate. "I won't book you. If it comes to that, I'll help you make a run for it. I'll run with you."

"You don't know what you're saying. You can't do that. It wouldn't only be the end of your career, you could wind up in jail yourself. Aiding and abetting a fugitive."

Delaney's gut felt like it was twisting. How could he ever go through the rest of his life without touching her, holding her, making love to her?

"It won't come to that. We'll nail the bastard who killed Nelson," he said vehemently, crushing her against him.

She buried her face into the crook of his shoulder. There was still her plan. It might not smoke out the murderer. And if it did, there was no guarantee she and Delaney would nab him before he "nabbed" her. A soft moan of fear escaped her lips.

"Marry me, Rachel."

Her head shot up. "What . . . ?"

"We can get the blood tests while we're in Philly, tie the knot this weekend. What do you say, Rachel?"

She shook her head so vigorously her curls flew all over the place. "No. No, I can't marry you, Del."

"Rachel, your baby deserves a father. I want to be its father. I want us to make a slew of brothers and sisters for it to play with."

"Del, you're crazy. We've known each other all of a couple of weeks. You still can't know for sure that I'm not a murderer. Or is it murderess?"

"I know it in my heart, Rachel."

"It's not enough."

"It is for me."

She pressed her cheek against his cheek. "It isn't for me. And it wouldn't be for you, either. You've got a lover's heart, Del, but a cop's mind. You can't split yourself in two. You can't separate your mind from your heart. Unless we can prove my innocence beyond a shadow of a doubt . . ."

"We'll prove it. We will. We will." As he assured her, he pulled the oversize T-shirt over her head. She was naked beneath, her breasts a bit fuller and more voluptuous now than just a few days ago. Her chest heaved, her rosy nipples tilting invitingly toward him. A priceless offering. He cupped her breasts, brushing his lips against her taut nipples, the tip of his tongue darting out to sample their delectable sweetness.

A quick, strumming heat spread through Rachel. Delaney began to touch her all over, setting off tiny electrical charges against her bare skin, soothing and arousing her at the same time. This was what she wanted—even if it was crazy, dangerous, had no future. She had to grab the moment. Her eyes fluttered closed. Tiny sparkling stars danced behind her eyelids.

Delaney quickly wriggled out of his jeans and shrugged off the shirt he was glad he hadn't bothered to button before coming into Rachel's room. Naked, he flung back the covers and crawled into his bed next to her. They were both too far gone for foreplay. The minute their bodies touched, they ignited. Rachel guided him on top of her, thinking even as he entered her that this might be the last time....

DELANEY WOKE WITH a start. A bad dream. He was suffocating. Only here he was awake and he still couldn't breathe. It took a few moments for his brain to reactivate.

Smoke. Cloying, billowing, choking him. The place was on fire.

Rachel. His hand shot out. He shook her. "Rachel. Rachel, wake up."

She didn't move.

He flung the covers off, coughing, gagging. He could hear the timbers sizzling around him, faintly make out through the thick blanket of smoke, the licks of flame dancing up the walls.

"Rachel." He shook her more vigorously. She wasn't asleep. She was past sleep. Unconscious. He pulled her deadweight to the floor. *Keep low. Got to keep low.*

The window was about ten feet away. It could have been ten miles. He tugged the cover and top sheet off the bed, threw one over Rachel, one over himself.

As he dragged her toward the window, she half came to. "What's . . . happening?"

Before he could tell her, she was out cold again. He wasn't in great shape himself—his lungs burning, his eyes tearing so much he couldn't see more than an inch or two in front of him.

It was probably only a couple of minutes before he got them to the window, but it felt like forever. He used all the strength he could muster to raise the window, gulping in fresh air.

"Okay, baby. We're almost home free," he said as he hoisted her up and out, grateful that this wasn't a second-story bedroom. He climbed out after her and dragged her away from the house.

A few minutes in the fresh air revived Rachel, but all she could do was look on in stunned silence at the burning house as she sat huddled in her blanket on the grass, with Delaney close beside her.

They could hear fire engines in the distance. One of the neighbors must have seen the smoke.

"You don't think it was an accident, do you?" she asked him.

Delaney shook his head slowly, cursing himself for having fallen asleep on the job.

LYLE WOODRUM GOT the report from the fire chief the next morning, confirming what Delaney and Rachel already knew. The fire had been deliberately started. The big question was, Who had started it? No one had a clue.

Woodrum had more bad news for them. "Your chief, Mendez, phoned this morning. He said he tried to reach you, but your phone was dead."

Delaney smiled wryly. Burned to a crisp was more to the point. "What did he want?"

Woodrum hesitated, his gaze skidding off Rachel's face.

Even before he said another word, they both knew.

"The bastard," Delaney muttered. "He swore he'd give me to the end of the week."

"He told me that Jonathan Thomas's alibi held. There's nothing to connect him in any way to Lang's murder." The chief ran his fingers through his sparse brown hair. "They're gonna book her and hold her for arraignment until Thursday." He gave Rachel a sympathetic look. "I've got a son-in-law who's a lawyer in the city. He doesn't do criminal law, but I'm sure he could recommend someone who'd be top-notch."

Rachel didn't say anything. She just sat there, numb. This was it. The moment she'd been dreading.

There was absolute silence. Delaney's hand reached for Rachel. Her lips compressed. Fighting back tears, she extended both of her arms as she felt his touch.

He looked at her. "What are you doing?"

"Don't you have to . . . cuff me?"

His hands went to his face. "No," he muttered.

Rachel dropped her arms to her lap. "We'd better get this over with." She was being very brave.

Delaney jumped up. "Yeah. You're right." He gave Woodrum a little nod and grabbed Rachel by the elbow.

Rachel rose, disconcerted by Delaney's cool manner. Well, he was a professional. She'd never really doubted he'd perform his duty if it came to that.

She looked back at the chief as Delaney hustled her toward the door. "Will you tell Kate and let her break it to my dad and . . . the others?"

Woodrum nodded. "I'm sorry, Rachel. You know we'll all be rooting for you. If there's anything I can do . . ."

"AREN'T WE TAKING the train into New York?" Rachel asked, as Delaney led her down the street from the police station to a car-rental place.

"No," he said brusquely.

"But . . ."

He looked at her. "We're not going to New York. We're going to Philly, remember?"

"But that was before—" It took a minute for the full impact of what Delaney was suggesting to hit her.

THEY PULLED OUT OF THE rental lot in a nondescript black Chevy sedan.

"What's the point now, Del? It's too late. It's over. What are we really going to find in Philly?"

"The murderer, I hope."

"And . . . if we don't?"

Delaney stared straight ahead out the windshield, his expression grim. He didn't answer. He just kept driving.

"I can't let you do this, Del. Please drive me to New York."

"I figure we'll be there in time for Suzanne's first show. I'll check her dressing room while she's onstage. If I come up empty-handed, I'll go on to her apartment."

"And what do I do?"

"Sit tight and stay out of sight."

Rachel clutched her hands together. They were trembling and clammy. "If you don't come up with anything, you're bringing me in, Del. There's no other choice."

"I'll come up with something," he said resolutely.

April 12

This is the worst. First Delaney's house is burned to the ground, then a warrant is issued for Aunt Rachel's arrest for the murder of Nelson Lang and then, a couple of hours ago, my mom and Chief Woodrum show up at school along with this detective from New York City to question me as to whether I have any idea where Delaney and Aunt Rachel might have gone.

It turns out my aunt's *on the lam!* A fugitive from justice. The cop from New York seems to think Aunt Rachel gave Delaney the slip and took off, and that now he's out hunting her down.

Boy, if he'd seen the way Delaney was kissing Aunt Rachel last night, I bet he'd be singing a different tune. I'm absolutely positive Delaney and my aunt ran off together. They're probably in Mexico this very minute.

Okay, it's real romantic and all, but what about us? Me? Mom? Grandpa Leo? Aunt Julie? Of course, Mom called Aunt Julie first thing. Oh, and Ben Sandler had an idea. He thought we should all go on television and make a plea for Aunt Rachel to turn herself in because it'll only be worse for her if she's caught. And that cop who came up from New York today acted like she would be caught, all right.

If only I could think of some way to prove Aunt Rachel's innocent. I think I'll bike on down to the old Seymour place again—well, what's left of it after the fire. If I could get a lead on the arsonist, I'd bet anything I'd have a lead on the murderer. When I told that to the cop from New York, he actually had the nerve to pat me on the head and ask me if I wanted to grow up to be Nancy Drew. As my mom would say, *Men!*

10

THE SHOW AT BOTTOMS UP in downtown Philly was in full swing when Delaney and Rachel arrived. Much against his better judgment, Delaney had let Rachel talk him into letting her tag along instead of holing up in their hotel room where they were registered under a phony name.

A dark, voluptuous beauty was in the middle of her act—a fanciful little routine in which she danced up and down the runway à la Ginger Rogers. Except that she was naked save for the G-string, top hat and tap shoes.

The audience, mostly men, showed their appreciation of the dancer's talents with loud cheers, whistles and catcalls. A few fellows close to the stage were eager to demonstrate their appreciation more concretely, but a couple of ex-linebacker types serving as bouncers made it clear that they could look but they couldn't touch.

Delaney guided Rachel to a dime-size table in the back of the dimly lit club. He started to order a couple of beers and then remembered alcohol was taboo for his pregnant companion. He got himself a beer and a ginger ale for Rachel.

"Why not just go ahead and order me a Shirley Temple?" Rachel quipped.

"Listen, I was the one—"

"You think that's Suzanne?"

Delaney gave the stripper a quick look. "No. She's a blonde. It was in the police report."

"She could be wearing a wig." Just as Rachel said that, the stripper dropped her head to her knees, her back—and backside—to the audience, her hair tumbling down to the floor as she shook her head back and forth to the pulsating hard-rock sound. "Mmm, I guess it's not a wig," Rachel concluded, feeling the heat rise in her face. "She's . . . good, isn't she?"

Delaney gave a noncommittal grunt. Of all the places on earth he'd have liked to be with Rachel, being in a strip joint with her wasn't one of them.

The tap-dancing stripper sashayed offstage, the lights dimmed, the music switched from rock to a twangy Arabic beat. When the lights came up on the stage, a luscious blonde was doing Salome's dance of the seven veils. An offstage announcer introduced their "Salome" as Suzanne English.

Delaney got up. "I'll be back in a few minutes."

Rachel gripped his sleeve. "Be careful."

"Stay put."

As he threaded his way through the crowd, Rachel watched the undulating Suzanne discard her first veil, then her second, her third . . .

In the end, the only veil left on was the one that concealed her nose and mouth so that Rachel never got a good look at her. There was no way to say she recognized Nelson's other jilted paramour, but Rachel got the oddest feeling watching her. There was something in the woman's eyes, or just her presence . . . It was as if she'd seen her before.

Rachel was a nervous wreck as the act drew to a close and Delaney hadn't returned. If he didn't hurry, he might collide with Suzanne in her dressing room.

She searched the cheering crowd. No sign of Delaney. Someone familiar, however, did catch her eye. Chief Louis Mendez of the NYPD. Fortunately, he hadn't spotted her. Yet.

RACHEL BREATHLESSLY hurried backstage to search for Delaney. She was turning down a passageway and nearly collided with one of the strippers. Rachel gasped, thinking at first that the blonde in the slinky red kimono robe was none other than Suzanne until a short, stubby-looking fellow who had an oversize cigar embedded between thin lips came up behind her, called her Valene, and said, "Hustle your buns, baby. You're on next."

Rachel breathed a sigh of relief when she spotted Delaney popping out of one of the dressing rooms. He didn't look nearly as happy to see her.

"I told you to sit tight," he said, grabbing her arm.

"A friend of ours is out there."

Delaney was in no mood for guessing games. "Who?"

"Your chief."

"Mendez? Oh, great." He spotted a fire exit at the end of the hall. "Come on."

Rachel didn't budge.

"Did you find anything?" she asked.

"No. We'll check out her apartment. Let's get out of here before Mendez comes backstage."

"It's no good, Del. I'm sure he's got men posted at her apartment building. If I show up there . . ."

"You're right."

"I knew you'd come to your senses."

"I'll do better on my own. I'll put you in a cab and you go straight back to the hotel and wait for me."

THERE WAS NO ARGUING with Delaney. He led Rachel out of the club via the fire exit and down a series of back alleys to a side street where he hailed her a cab. As soon as the cab pulled out and he knew Rachel was safely off, Delaney backtracked to his car, spotting Mendez step out into the street to check with the two Philly cops who were staked out in an unmarked cruiser in front of the strip joint. He ducked into a doorway until Mendez got into the cruiser and drove away. Then he made a run for his car and headed straight for Suzanne English's address, trying not to think about what was going to happen if he came up empty-handed there, too. As it was, even if he found the letter, it wouldn't be enough to get Rachel off the hook. Suzanne English still had an ironclad alibi for the night of the murder. And there was a damn good chance she was no more guilty than Rachel.

YEARS OF EXPERIENCE made it relatively easy for Delaney to slip into Suzanne English's building undetected. Her apartment was on the top floor, a small but classy penthouse suite. Delaney wondered if the stripper would have to find new, less sumptuous quarters now that Lang, who'd footed the bill, was dead? There were certainly no signs of Suzanne packing up. Maybe she'd found herself someone to replace Lang.

He started going systematically through the apartment, working his way from her bedroom with its huge king-size bed and red brocade wallpaper, to the living room and kitchen. Nothing. He went back up to the bedroom. He looked all around, then came back to the thickly tufted white-satin-covered headboard. He crossed over to it for a closer look—especially at the upper right-hand corner, where the tacks holding the material in place protruded slightly.

Delaney yanked them out, pulling back the material. Something fell onto the pillows. It was Lang's notebook. Delaney went to snap it up. And for the second time, no sooner had he got his hands on the book, than everything went black....

EVERYTHING WAS BLURRY, but one face slowly came into focus.

"Mendez," Delaney croaked, wincing as his hand went up to the lump at the back of his head. "Jeez, what'd you hit me with, anyway?"

"I didn't hit you," Mendez snapped. "Although, believe me, if I thought it would knock some sense into you..."

Another familiar face popped into Delaney's line of sight. He shook his head even though it hurt like hell. "Rachel."

"I'm sorry, Del. I know you told me to go back to the hotel, but when the cab drove by the club, guess who I saw coming out the door?"

Seeing that Delaney was in no mood for guessing games, she hurried on. "Thomas. I saw Jonathan

Thomas. He got into a nifty little sports coupe and drove off."

Delaney raised a hand. "Don't tell me. You told the cabbie to follow him."

"Right to this address."

Delaney looked over at Mendez. "And right into your waiting arms."

"Sorry, Delaney."

Delaney's gaze shifted back to Rachel. This time he saw the handcuffs. And the two plainclothes cops on either side of her.

"I don't suppose you nabbed Thomas, as well," Delaney asked his chief.

"You were in here all by your lonesome when we got here."

Delaney cursed under his breath.

There was a commotion in the next room. Suzanne English, followed by a beefy male companion, strode into her bedroom. "What the hell is going on here?" she demanded, sweeping a look of outraged indignation past all of them.

AFTER AN EXHAUSTING and lengthy meeting with her lawyer, all Rachel really wanted to do was curl up on the sofa in the courtroom office and sleep the two hours until her arraignment. Instead, she sat there with Delaney, and the two of them tried to figure it all out.

"She had the notebook," Delaney was saying. "So that hood driving around in the blue sedan must have been working for her."

"That character who came into her bedroom with her fits Skye's description. Tall, bulky, dark hair." She sighed. "Like that wouldn't fit the description of half the men in the whole country."

Delaney reached out for her hand. "Don't be discouraged, Rachel. I think we may be on to something here."

"What I can't figure out is how Thomas knew Suzanne had the notebook," Rachel said. And then she snapped her fingers. "Wait. What if she told him. What if she was using the notebook to blackmail him."

Delaney beamed at her. "Beautiful and smart, to boot. How did I ever get so lucky?"

"Some luck," Rachel said glumly.

"Come on. Keep thinking," he prodded, as much to keep her spirits up as for her to hit upon something that might trigger an idea in his mind. He was desperate for an idea; desperate to produce some hard evidence that would keep Rachel from being arraigned for Lang's murder. All they had was circumstantial evidence against her, but as it stood now, it was probably strong enough to win the DA a trial.

Delaney rose and started to pace. "Let's work our way back," he said. "Suzanne had the notebook. Her pal could very well have been the goon who swiped it from me. She probably sent him out to Pittsville to make sure you hadn't taken anything from Lang that could tie her into the murder."

"You really think she murdered Lang?"

"She had the same motive you had. Let's say she gets that letter from Lang and she's fit to be tied. Or she thinks she can sweet-talk him back into the relationship. She shows up just when you're heading out of the building, waits for you to disappear, then goes up to see him. Would he let her in? Sure, he would. Which explains why there was no sign of a forced entry. She pleads with him not to dump her. He doesn't come around and she stabs him in the back."

"She does look like the kind of woman who could stab someone in the back," Rachel conceded. "But there's just one little problem. At the time Nelson was murdered she was onstage at the Bottoms Up, probably doing her dance of the seven veils." Rachel shot a look at Delaney.

"What?" he asked.

She blinked several times, her mind spinning. "Del, I think I may be on to something. I think I know how Suzanne could have been in two places at the same time."

THE COURTROOM WAS filled to overflowing with the residents of Pittsville. Everyone was there—Rachel's two sisters, her niece Skye, her father and Mellie, Ben Sandler, Meg Cromwell, and scores of neighbors, friends and well-wishers.

As he had since the arraignment hearing first began, the judge once again banged his gavel to quiet everyone, threatening to clear the court if there wasn't absolute order.

Rachel sat beside her lawyer, Neal Logan, whom Chief Woodrum's son had highly recommended. Logan was in his early thirties, very poised and self-confident. "I'd like to call Martha Munson, also known as Valene Parrish, to the stand."

The blond stripper from the Bottoms Up Club nervously approached the stand. Even with clothes on—

a hip-hugging red linen shift—Valene's claim to fame was quite apparent.

After she was sworn in, Rachel's lawyer rose from his chair and walked over to her. He gave her a reassuring smile. "Now, Miss Munson . . ."

"You can call me . . . Valene," the stripper said with a nervous smile.

Logan nodded pleasantly. "Valene, would you tell the court what happened on the night of March 14."

"When exactly do you want me to start?"

"How about starting with Suzanne English's request," he said, cutting to the chase.

Rachel turned to Delaney, who was sitting right behind her. He put a reassuring hand on her shoulder. She placed her hand over his.

"Well," Valene said breathily. "Suzanne asked me if I'd mind doing her Salome number for her. She knew I was having a little problem with some nasty creditors and she offered me a nice piece of change. . . ."

"How much?" Logan asked.

"A thousand bucks."

"She paid you a thousand dollars to go on for her that night?"

Valene dabbed at her mouth with a hankie. "She said she had a hot date, and no one would know the difference because we've both got blond hair and it's a snap for me to wear it the way she does. And with the veil over my face and all, no one would know the difference."

"You mean," Logan said slowly, "that the audience would assume it was Suzanne English up there onstage doing that routine?"

"Everyone thought it was Suzanne," Valene replied. "Even Nicky, the stage manager, didn't get wind of it. He would have fired Suzanne if he'd found out. He's a real bastard. Can I say that word here?"

Logan smiled. "Yes, that's fine, Valene."

"He would have probably canned me, too. Which was why I didn't say anything."

"Is that the only reason?" Logan queried.

"Well . . . the next day Suzanne did give me another thousand bucks after I swore I'd never breathe a word." Valene's eyes shot to Suzanne English who was sitting rigidly in the second-row aisle seat. "It's not like I swore on a Bible or nothing."

"Thank you, Miss Munson . . . Valene. That will be all."

That was all from Valene, but there was still more to come. Neal Logan entered into evidence a rhinestone earring that had been found at the scene of the fire at the old Seymour place. Kate put her arm around her daughter and hugged her close. Skye beamed. She was the one who'd found it amid the ashes and charred ruins.

Delaney had reason to beam, too. He'd found the match to the earring in Suzanne's jewelry box in Philly.

The best dramatic moment came when Suzanne English burst into tears and shouted out a confession right there in the courtroom. Sobbing, she claimed that she'd killed Nelson in self-defense, swearing that he'd threatened her and was reaching for something to strike her with when she picked up the knife and stabbed him in the back. Suzanne was immediately remanded into custody and Rachel was cleared of all charges.

Everyone cheered.

Mendez, who was seated beside Delaney, grinned at him. "So, now I suppose you'll be asking for a raise."

"No. A transfer," Delaney said, climbing over the railing and pulling an ecstatic Rachel into his arms. "To Pittsville."

"What?"

Delaney and Rachel were already wrapped in each other's arms as the delighted folk of Pittsville cheered and flocked around them.

Kelso came up beside Mendez. "I think you just went and lost one of your best men."

Mendez sighed. "Hell, it's about time he settled down."

Delaney caught the last bit of his chief's remark and gently drew Rachel from him, but continued to hold on to her. "What do you say, Rachel? Will you marry me?"

Breathless with excitement and relief, Rachel kissed him hard on the mouth. "When?"

He looked around at her family, friends and neighbors gathered all around them. Mellie Oberchon winked at him.

"What about right now? Everyone's here. We've even got a judge...."

May 1

Just got a card from Aunt Rachel and Delaney. They're having a great time on their honeymoon in Bermuda. Mom and Grandpa are planning a big party for them when they get back. Aunt Julie's flying in for it. I can't believe they're actually going to settle right here in

Pittsville when they could live anywhere they wanted to. Aunt Rachel seems to think this is the best place to raise kids. I gather from what I overheard Mom and Aunt Julie talking about on the phone, that Aunt Rachel and Delaney plan to have a lot of kids. And guess who's going to get asked to baby-sit!

I don't really mind, though. They'll probably have neat kids. And just to clear the decks, as Grandpa Leo says, I guess the truth is I did have sort of a crush on Delaney for a while, there. Not now that he's my uncle, not to mention Pittsville's new police chief, now that Lyle Woodrum's decided to try his hand at real estate. Before he left his post, though, he did give me a special citation of merit for my help in the investigation of the Nelson Lang murder. I hung it up right next to my Bon Jovi poster.

Well, things are back to being dull again in beautiful downtown Pittsville, but at least summer's not too far off. There's the phone. I'd better go get it....

May 1 (cont.)

Hold on to your hats. Something's up. Mom just got off the phone with Aunt Julie. Aunt Julie got canned! All Mom would tell me was that it had something to do with her having filled in too many missing blanks and having embarrassed a very influential senator right on the air. And it turned out that the senator was best college buddies with the producer of "News and Views," the show Aunt Julie hosts with her boyfriend Jordan Hammond. Or, I should say, *hosted*. Hmm. I wonder if Jordan will quit in protest. I certainly think he should.

Anyway, Aunt Julie's coming back to Pittsville for the summer. To lick her wounds, Mom told Ben Sandler, who stopped by the house. He didn't seem particularly broken up about Aunt Julie getting the sack and "returning to her roots," as he put it. He even told Mom he wouldn't mind having Aunt Julie cohost "Pittsville Patter" with him. Boy, did Mom crack up.

Anyway, this summer may not turn out to be as dull as I thought. Stay tuned . . .

* * * * *

Look for Julie Hart's story in
HEARTSTRUCK,
available in September 1995 from Temptation.

Temptation
brings you...

Bestselling Temptation author Elise Title is back with a funny, sexy, three-part mini-series. **The Hart Girls** follows the ups and downs of three feisty, independent sisters who work at a TV station in Pittsville, New York.

In **Dangerous at Heart (Temptation August '95)**, a dumbfounded Rachel Hart can't believe she's a suspect in her ex-fiancé's death. She only dumped Nelson—she didn't bump him off! Sexy, hard-edged cop Delaney Parker must uncover the truth—or bring Rachel in.

Look out for Julie Hart's story in **Heartstruck (Temptation September '95)**. Kate Hart's tale, **Heart to Heart**, completes this wonderful trilogy in October '95.

Spoil yourself next month
with these four novels from

Temptation

HEARTSTRUCK by Elise Title

Second in *The Hart Girls* trilogy

Julie Hart had reluctantly agreed to co-host a TV talk show
with heart-throb Ben Sandler. The ratings soared as she
challenged the guests and even ended up hitting the charming
Ben! But there was no denying the chemistry between them,
both on *and off* the set.

MAD ABOUT YOU by Alyssa Dean

Faye—an innocent, lost in the big city—had charmed Kent
MacIntyre, until she had stolen his files. He found her hiding
place only to learn that she desperately needed his help. A
world-weary, cynical investigator, Kent knew damn well not to
trust any woman. Why did he so want to believe her?

UNDERCOVER BABY by Gina Wilkins

Detective Dallas Sanders had taken part in some unusual
undercover operations, but cracking the baby-smuggling ring
was the toughest. Especially since it meant playing the part of
an unwed, pregnant woman. Even worse, she had to pretend to
be head over heels in love with no-good Sam Perry.

PLAYBOY McCOY by Glenda Sanders

Laurel Randolph had all the "facts" on McCoy. But she pushed
aside any nagging doubts when she embarked on a shipboard
fling with him. Under the hot tropical sun, McCoy made her
feel sexy...desirable...loved. But was it the real thing?

A years supply of Mills & Boon romances — absolutely free!

Would you like to win a years supply of heartwarming and passionate romances? Well, you can and they're FREE! All you have to do is complete the word puzzle below and send it to us by 29th February 1996. The first 5 correct entries picked out of the bag after that date will win a years supply of Mills & Boon romances (six books every month—worth over £100). What could be easier?

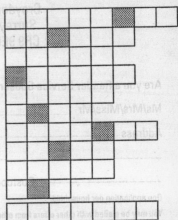

GMWIMSIN

NNSAUT

ACEHB

EMSMUR

ANCOE

DNSA

RTOISTU

THEOL

ATYCH

NSU

MYSTERY DESTINATION

Please turn over for details on how to enter

How to enter

Simply sort out the jumbled letters to make ten words all to do with being on holiday. Enter your answers in the grid, then unscramble the letters in the shaded squares to find out our mystery holiday destination.

After you have completed the word puzzle and found our mystery destination, don't forget to fill in your name and address in the space provided below and return this page in an envelope (you don't need a stamp). Competition ends 29th February 1996.

Mills & Boon Romance Holiday Competition
FREEPOST
P.O. Box 344
Croydon
Surrey
CR9 9EL

Are you a Reader Service Subscriber?   Yes ❑   No ❑

Ms/Mrs/Miss/Mr _____

Address _____

_____

_____ Postcode _____

One application per household.

You may be mailed with other offers from other reputable companies as a result of this application. If you would prefer not to receive such offers, please tick box. ❑

mps MAILING PREFERENCE SERVICE

COMP495
B